Up

in

Smoke

T.K. Chapin

EMBERS AND ASHES - BOOK 3

UP IN
SMOKE

Best Selling Author of "The Perfect Cast"
T.K. CHAPIN

Up in Smoke

ISBN-13:
978-1519399939

ISBN-10:
1519399936

DEDICATION

Dedicated to my mother,

the woman who taught me

that all things are possible with God.

CONTENTS

ACKNOWLEDGMENTS

First and foremost, I want to thank God. God's salvation through the death, burial and resurrection of Jesus Christ gives us all the ability to have a personal relationship with the creator of the Universe.

I also want to thank my wife. She's my muse and my inspiration. A wonderful wife, an amazing mother and the best person I have ever met. She's great and has always stood by me with every decision I have made along life's way.

I'd like to thank my editors and early readers for helping me along the way. I also want to thank all of my friends and extended family for the support. It's a true blessing to have every person I know in my life.

.

CHAPTER 1

With a trembling hand, I set the ink pen down on the desk in my study. My eyes lifted to the ceiling as I said a quiet but sincere prayer to the Lord. I prayed for peace I couldn't find, and comfort I couldn't hold. My prayers, while sincere, were lacking a certain depth. My once deep and meaningful conversations with my Creator had transformed into a 'To Do' list for God. I was writing a will, which terrified me, so I went to the one resource I knew that was able to help—God. My walk with the Lord had been strong in my younger years while I raised a family, but it had dwindled after my daughter had started her own life. It was a slow fade, with no exact date or time for when it all began sliding downhill, but I sensed that something wasn't right along the way.

Picking up the pen again, I sighed as I continued to string together the words that I knew would be read aloud when I was gone from this world. It was an unsettling thought, and it troubled me greatly to imagine a day when I wasn't alive.

"Rick," my wife, Susan, said as she opened the door to my study. She was a welcomed and pleasant interruption from the task at hand. I looked over at her.

"Yes, dear?" I asked, hoping it was time to leave.

"I've packed our bags and loaded them into the car. We can go whenever you're ready." Watching her, I saw her eyes fall to my desk and to the pen in my hand. "What are you doing?" she inquired as she stepped closer to me.

I swept a hand over the will and said, "Just some

paperwork."

She nodded, and her eyes saw my finished slice of watermelon sitting on the plate on my desk. She beamed as she reminisced. "Do you remember that delightful afternoon we had down by the lake? We'd found the perfect watermelon at the store to go along with our picnic."

I let myself join her in the reflection back to our youth. It was a time before we had our daughter, Bethany, back before we had any responsibilities in life. So many years ago, yet so easy to recall in my mind. I smiled as I looked over at her, and said, "I could almost taste that watermelon now."

Her smile softened as she looked out the window behind me at the falling rain outside. She let out a long breath and said, "I'll be downstairs waiting for you to finish up."

She headed for the door.

"I'm just going to wrap up here and then we can head out. Did you pack my blood pressure medicine?"

Stopping at the door, she looked back at me. Those eyes. They were beautiful. Even after thirty years of marriage, they were still able to touch the depths of my soul with such ease and precision. "I always do." A smile crept at the corner of my lips as I returned to writing. Susan knew me better than anyone else on the planet. She even knew me better than I knew myself. I still wondered how I was able to keep a secret from her, though. Maybe it was because the thought of her finding out that our savings had all but vanished terrified me more than even the worst of the fires I had seen in all my years as a firefighter. She was my other half, my soul mate, and my best friend. If she were to find out the truth, I was certain she would leave me. I couldn't take that. I loved her, I needed her, and life without Susan wasn't a life worth having.

As I wrote down into words that my cousin Jeffery back in Arkansas would be getting the cigar boxes and baseball cards after I pass onto glory, I could feel my anxiety rising. *I can't do this right now*, I thought to myself, closing my eyes for a moment. Opening up the desk drawer, I set the will inside and shut it. *There's plenty of time to write a will*, I thought to myself as I stood up. I don't care if

Captain Taylor feels that all of us at the station need to have one. I'm only fifty-three. Turning off the light as I left the room, I headed downstairs.

We got into the car outside and I turned the key over. Glancing over at Susan, I could tell something was off about her.

"What's wrong?" I asked, looking at her with raised eyebrows. Seeing her gag and cover her mouth, I said, "Go inside to the bathroom, dear."

She nodded and kept her mouth covered as she flung open the car door and booked it back up the driveway toward the house. Worried, I kept my eyes on her as I watched her open the door and rush inside.

While waiting for her to return, I thought about cancelling the trip altogether. Her lying in a hotel bed while feeling sick didn't sound like a good time for her. When Susan got back into the car, I asked, "Want to just cancel the trip and stay home?"

She shook her head as she dug into her purse for something. Pulling out a pack of gum, she took a stick out and popped it into her mouth. "I'll be okay, Rick. Let's go."

"You sure?" I asked, concerned.

She nodded and set her purse on the floor of the car, just beneath her seat. "Just get driving so we can get there before it gets too late. I want to eat at that restaurant inside the hotel, and they only have the discounted prime rib meal until six."

"What are you? Pregnant? You just yakked!" I shook my head, smiling. "How on earth could you think of food right now?"

She laughed. "I haven't been able to get pregnant in at least twenty years . . . you know that, Rick. I just love my prime rib!" She looked out the window.

"Besides, I feel better now."

"All right. If you say so!"

I put the car into reverse and backed out of the driveway. She always had an appetite when it came to prime rib. I was pretty confident that even on her deathbed she'd be willing to get up if it meant she would get to eat prime rib.

"How much are you thinking?" she asked as we came up on our exit on the freeway.

"The usual," I replied.

"Two hundred?" she asked.

"Yeah," I replied.

"Okay."

We always agreed on a set amount to spend at the casino before we got there. There wasn't any pride in my gambling. I knew it wasn't exactly the right thing to be doing as a born-again Christian, but I enjoyed it. I wrote the time off as entertainment. It was a date night for us, I'd tell myself. It builds our relationship, I'd insist to myself. Some people went to movies, some had expensive cars, and we had the casino.

Arriving at our hotel room on the fourth floor of the North Bend Casino and Resort, I set our bags down on the floor, near the corner of the room. The heater suddenly kicked on, and I looked over to see Susan tinkering with the thermostat.

"It's fine in here, don't turn it on," I said, going over toward her.

"It's freezing!" she insisted.

"Compared to what?" I asked. "We don't keep the

thermostat higher than 70 degrees at home."

"It's a vacation, Rick. You don't have to worry about the bill here." She smiled as she headed into the bathroom. "You ready to go eat?" she shouted from behind the door.

I lay down on the bed and kicked my shoes off, expecting her to take a while getting ready. I grabbed the remote and called back to her, "Yeah, we can go whenever." Turning on the TV, I began to endlessly flip through the channels.

Not even five minutes later, she came out of the bathroom and was ready to go. "Aren't we leaving?" she asked.

"Yeah. I didn't know how long it was going to take you, dear." Turning my eyes back to the TV, I shut it off and got up from the bed.

Out in the hallway, Susan's eyes filled with excitement as we headed toward the elevators. I grabbed her hand and pulled her close to me. As we walked, I sang softly into her ear, "Have I told you lately that I love you?" Susan began to hum along with me.

Susan was my only true love, the mother of our

child, and my best friend. Everything in the world could fall apart without affecting me, but if I didn't have her, I'd have nothing.

After dinner, as we were going back into our room, Susan grabbed her stomach with one hand and hit a wall with the other to hold herself up. "Ahhh . . ." She moaned as she bent over.

"Your stomach? I thought you felt better. Maybe eating wasn't such a good idea."

"Quit talking about it and help me, please . . ." she whimpered as she leaned into the wall. My steps shuffled over to her, and I grabbed her arm to help her to the bed. Suddenly, she breathed a few quick breaths and then ran into the bathroom. Cringing at the sounds on the other side of the bathroom door, I leaned against the door and waited a few moments for her to come out. Then, I lay down on the bed and turned on the TV.

Sometime later—it's hard to say exactly when— Susan came out of the bathroom. She looked like death as she wobbled over to the bed and crash landed face-first into a pillow. Her hair was frazzled and her eyes drooped. She looked exhausted.

"You need anything?" I asked.

She stayed silent, which was rare. I knew whatever she had going on was bad.

I got up from the bed and went over to our bags on the floor. Opening up the duffle bag, I grabbed her favorite blanket she'd had for nearly a decade and covered her up. Lying back down on my side of the bed, I continued to watch the 1984 World Series on the classic sports channel.

Susan raised her face up from the pillow and pushed back a few strands of hair from her eyes. "Just go, dear," she said, before collapsing her head back into the pillow.

"What?"

"Just go play," she said in a muffled voice from the pillow. "I'm not going to be playing tonight, honey. I'm sorry."

I turned off the TV and sat up, turning toward her. "I'm sorry you're not feeling well, dear. I want to stay here with you in case you need anything. I don't need to play."

"Go play. I want to lie in silence and rest," she replied.

Okay. Getting off the bed, I grabbed a room key from the desk below the TV and came around to her side of the bed. Bending my knees slightly, I pulled her mess of hair back behind her ear and kissed her cheek.

"Win big," she said in a sickly tone, trying to sound enthused.

I smiled. Brushing my fingers through her hair, I asked, "Do you want a soda or anything before I leave?"

She looked at me with one eye closed. "That'd be great, dear."

I nodded. "Okay. I'll be right back."

Returning a few minutes later, I poured her a cup of the lemon-lime soda I got from the vending machine down the hall and put a straw in it. I set it next to her on the night stand.

"Dear . . ." I said in a soft whisper to see if she was awake.

No response. She was already out cold.

I bent over the bed and kissed her forehead once more. "I love you," I said. Tip-toeing as quietly as possible, I headed out of the room and down the hallway to the elevators.

CHAPTER 2

Taking a long drink of my soda, I continued my

efforts to read the kid sitting across from me. He

was a tough one to figure out. He wasn't like the old

guy to my left in the ten-gallon cowboy hat that only

bet when he had a good hand. There was also no

similarity between him and the punk rocker guy to

my right, who had more piercings in his face than I

thought was humanly possible. The punk would

bluff when he got in too deep, and he had an easy

tell that I picked up on early. He'd sniff every time he was bluffing. This kid, on the other hand, had no tells that I could pick up on. He showed zero emotion. I liked to think that I'd gotten pretty good at reading people over the years, but he had been at this table with me for a while and I still couldn't figure him out. All the kid would do is pop an earbud in and out of his ear when someone would talk to him.

Glancing at my cards once more—a king and a ten—I narrowed my eyes on the kid. Our eyes met for a moment, but he looked away. My eyes fell on the three cards from the flop that was already on the table: ace of hearts, ten of clubs, eight of diamonds.

"What's your name, kid?" I asked.

"Robert," he replied.

"What you listening to, Robert?" I asked.

He furrowed his eyebrows. "Jazz," he said curtly.

Our dealer, Joe, said, "Get on with the game. You guys can chat later."

I checked.

"Raise," the kid said, tossing in fifty dollars' worth of poker chips toward the middle of the table. The dealer pulled the chips into the middle of the table and I looked over at Robert. He remained as cold as ice, with no tells.

His fifty dollar raise was going to put me all in. My night would be over if I lost this hand. My eyes shifted to my few remaining poker chips that sat on the table next to me.

I rubbed the back of my neck as the decision to go all-in plagued my mind. It was quite early into my evening, and if I lost it all in one hand, I'd be forced to end my casino venture quite early. I glanced at my watch. It was only eight o'clock. I looked over at the kid as he seemed to get lost in his music once again. Staring at the three cards that were already on the table, I thought back to thirty or so minutes ago when the kid bluffed me.

The last time we ended up head-to-head, I folded in the fear that he had something better than I did. The kid was weird and revealed his hand instead of mucking. He had a high card of a jack, nothing else. I had folded two pairs, and I would have won. He'd show his cards whether he had a hand or not—that tactic kept me guessing each and every hand he'd play.

"Call," I replied, coming out of my thoughts. Pushing my chair out, I stood up and crossed my arms. He flipped over an ace and a queen. He wasn't bluffing this time. He had the high pair with his ace matching the ace on the flop. My heart began to pound inside my chest. It was so strong I could feel it in my ears. My anxiety climbed and my breath became short. Waiting for the last two cards—the turn and the river—to fall was pure torture.

The turn came: two of clubs.

The river came: ace of diamonds.

That was it—I was broke. Reaching across the table, I shook his hand and said, "Well done, kid."

"You played some good poker," he replied, popping his earbud out as we shook hands. "What's your name?"

"I'm Rick, but everyone around here knows me as Blaze."

His eyebrows shot up. "Why Blaze?" he asked. "You a legend or something?"

"No legend. I'm a firefighter. Down in Spokane," I replied.

"Right on. Well, good luck. Hope we cross paths again."

"Good luck to you," I said, pushing in my chair to leave.

Grabbing my cup of soda from the table, I turned and began to leave the casino floor, heading back toward the hotel lobby. As I walked, I kept my eyes glued to the funky floral carpet design, trying to keep my mind occupied by going over the pattern I had seen so many times before. Then it happened, like it always did: the lights of the slot machines danced in my peripherals, and the sounds of them gnawed at my consciousness.

I wanted to stay. I wanted to play longer. I needed to.

I checked the time on my watch. It was eight thirty, far too early to call it a night. *Susan's already asleep, and I'm not going to sleep well*, I told myself as I slowed my pace to a stop. Lifting my eyes up from the carpet, I saw it, like it was put there just for me. The ATM.

Just a little longer to play, I told myself. What's the point of coming up to a casino for the weekend if you aren't going to have fun? Bills are paid. My daughter is well-off enough to take care of herself and the grandkids. The fire station's pension plan is more than enough for retirement. What's the hurt to spend a little more? I thought of Susan. What would she think?

My conscience reminded me that she *told* me to play.

I looked back at the ATM.

Just a little more, my conscience urged me on.

Going over to the ATM, I pulled out my wallet and slid out the debit card—not the one to our regular checking account. I made sure it was the one tied to our savings account over at the Credit Union. I slid it through the card reader.

The screen read, *Balance: $11,000.*

I sighed as I went through the menus and thought about the last three years. I've wasted almost seventy thousand dollars on poker at this blasted casino. Mostly competitions, but each time I played, I was filled with regret. It was never enough to stop me, though.

This was my soul crushing secret. I, Rick Alderman,

was addicted to gambling. I had singlehandedly cut our savings and my inheritance by more than half because of my inability to tell myself *No*.

If Susan knew **the truth,** there was no doubt in my mind that it'd ruin our relationship—our whole marriage. She adored me and thought I was incapable of wrongdoing . . . well, outside of leaving my socks turned inside-out and my boots on the carpet. After thirty years of marriage, with its ups and downs, blessings and failures, this would be the one thing we couldn't bounce back from, and I knew it. But even knowing that didn't stop me. I justified my sin. After all, I had worked for a portion of that money, and the remainder was from my inheritance. The ATM did its part and spat out the five hundred dollars I told it to. *This time I'll win*, I thought to myself as I turned and headed back to the same poker table. Another way I justified my behavior was by thinking that if I could get on a good winning streak, I could earn all that money back and she'd never have to know. I would never have to break her heart.

Arriving back at the table, I was pleased to see that

Robert was still there.

"Welcome back, Blaze," the kid said, grinning from across the table as he rolled a poker chip between his fingers on one hand.

The corner of my mouth hinted at a smile as I pulled the chips Joe gave me over to my spot on the table. I had been coming to Joe's table for years. He was really the only one who knew the real state of my addiction. "I came to take my money back, plus yours," I said to Robert.

"Confident," the kid replied. He looked over at the cowboy as he continued, "Larry here was telling me that you played in the Horseshoe Tournament a while back."

"You heard right. I placed fourth, right outside of the bubble for a prize. Didn't earn a dime." My words were heavy as I thought about the bad beat I had in the tournament.

"That ain't right," the kid replied as Joe began dealing us cards. I favored Joe the most out of all of the dealers at North Bend Casino because he was quiet, yet always kind and respectful. He didn't put up with the obnoxious drunks or jerks either. He wasn't like the other dealers who would take anyone inebriated just so they could make a few extra bucks in tips.

"It happens. The tourney only paid out the top three spots. I laughed a little as I continued, "Sometimes that's just how the cards fall."

"Yeah." As he looked at his cards, I took note of his lack of an earbud. Wasn't sure if he forgot or if it was because we were chatting.

He raised. This time, it was $100. Still no earbud. Peeking at my cards, I saw that I had a pair of aces—hearts and spades. There wasn't a hand that I hated more. I was never able to win with them, but I always felt an obsessive need to play them.

"Call," I said, tossing my chip into the middle of the table.

The flop came. It was a two of hearts, two of clubs and a queen of hearts.

The kid raised another hundred dollars' worth of chips. Then he grabbed his earbud that he hadn't had in and placed it into his ear. *That's his tell*, I thought to myself. He's bluffing. The kid focuses more on the music playing in his ear when he doesn't have anything. How did I not notice it before?

"Raise," I said. Tossing in the original hundred to call his, I followed it with another hundred dollars. He smiled at me and raised again, this time forcing me to go all-in.

Everything told me he was lying. He was pot committed and trying to scare me off. Without hesitation, I went all-in and stood up.

He removed his earbud and looked up at me.

"Really? First hand back and you're all-in?"

I grinned at him. I suspected that he was sweating bullets underneath that hard exterior.

He leaned in and looked at the flop for a moment and then called my all-in. "I'm sorry to do this to you, Blaze." He flipped a two of diamonds and a king of spades. He wasn't bluffing. My read was wrong. Flipping my two aces over, we both waited for the turn and the river.

Another queen came up on the turn, this time a diamond.

My heart raced for what felt like a million miles per hour as Joe turned over the River card. *Come on, please! An ace! Come on! Come on!* I rooted myself on internally.

Ace of clubs.

Shooting both my hands up into the air, I felt like I was on top of the world. "Congratulations," the kid said from across the table, smiling. "Won it on the river."

"Yep." Leaning across the table, I shook his hand and sat back down. Pulling the chips over to me, I began stacking them up. I was back in business. Up to a grand already, and the night was young.

The kid, the cowboy and I played for the next couple of hours at that table. My stack went up and down like waves in an ocean: up one hour, down the next. As we approached the three o'clock hour that next morning, I began to think of Susan and how she'd be getting up in a mere four hours or so. I needed to get back up to my room and get a little shut eye before she woke up. Folding my last hand and electing not to play, I said to the kid, "I'm calling it a night."

"It's been a pleasure." His eyes watched me as I loaded the poker chip holder with my winnings to leave.

Taking my chips, I stood up and headed over to the cage to cash them in. As I waited for the cashier to tally them up, I felt a tap on my shoulder.

"Blaze," a familiar voice said from behind me.

"What's up?" I said, turning around. It was Robert.

"You have some serious skill. You should go down to Vegas next month and play in the World Series of Poker." He looked serious, but that didn't stop me from laughing.

I laughed, shaking my head. "I'm not that good, kid. I couldn't sit with those hall of fame poker players. Plus, everyone and their cousin tries to get in on that."

He shook his head. "I went a few years back. It's not like what you think. It's more than just one main event. They have multiple tournaments scattered across a three month window."

The idea sounded like a farfetched fantasy, but I entertained the thought for a moment. "What's the buy-in? You going?"

"Not this year. Ten grand for the one I played in when I went. It's one of the last tournaments they host every year. I believe it's on the twenty-ninth of this month."

I was about to respond, but the cashier caught my attention.

"Sir," the cashier said.

"Yeah?" I leaned up toward the cage.

"How would you like your payout?"

"Uh . . . in cash," I replied, distracted by the thought of the kid's proposition.

She laughed. "I mean, what bills would you like?"

"Hundreds is fine." My face went flush, I could feel it.

She counted it all out to me. All two thousand and fifty dollars of it. I was on top of the world. My eyes were wide as I scooped up the cash. "Thank you," I said to her. Turning, I left the cage and the kid followed beside me.

"Look at that. Two grand for the night. What'd you start with?"

I shrugged. "Two hundred and then another five."

He lightly pushed my shoulder, stopping me. "See that? You turned seven hundred dollars into two grand in one night. Vegas better watch out!"

"Yeah, but I rarely win like this. Vegas sounds like a

lot of fun, but I can't see it happening."

He nodded. "You broke or something?" he asked with his chin raised, almost looking a bit suspicious.

"Excuse me?" I snapped at him.

"Sorry." He shrugged slightly. "Just figured maybe I'm barking up the wrong tree. I don't want to waste my time working on getting you a free hotel stay if this isn't even a reality for you."

"No. I have money—plenty of it, kid—but I'm not sure about Vegas. I've been coming here for decades playing at my little five-man table. Seems extreme to go to Vegas." I didn't really have a ton of money, but I wasn't going to reveal that to some kid.

"I understand. Just think about it, *Blaze*. Last time I went, I placed sixth and walked away with a hundred grand."

His comment piqued my interest. That was a lot of dough for sixth place. "How many people bought in?"

"Three hundred," he replied.

That was a lot of people, but only two hundred more than what I was used to at North Bend. "I'll think about it, kid. Thanks."

Heading out of the casino, I hid the cash in my inside coat pocket so I could sneak it back into the bank before work on Monday without drawing any suspicion from Susan. I hid all but five hundred to show Susan. She'd be happy about it and I could put that portion back into checking. It was the only way I could share in the victory without mentioning that I took money from the other account.

As I rode the elevator up to my room in the hotel, I thought about Robert and that tournament in Vegas he had been talking about. *Ten thousand dollars is too much for one shot. But then again, that kid did walk away with a hundred grand.* The best I did in any of the tournaments was getting a buffet coupon. I didn't entirely discount the idea of going; there was a lot of possibility in it.

CHAPTER 3

Back at home two days later, my favorite smell in

the world tickled my nose as I came down the stairs,

causing me to crack a smile: bacon. Susan made me

breakfast the first morning of every work week. It

helped motivate me for the week of work ahead.

Coming into the kitchen with a smile, I walked to

her side and kissed her cheek.

"Finally feeling a bit better today, dear?" I asked as I

took a seat at the table. "I didn't hear you get up

once last night."

She brought over a plate of eggs and bacon and set it down in front of me. "Yes. Much better, thank you," she replied. "Coffee or orange juice?" she asked on her way back around the kitchen island.

"Coffee, please," I replied, bowing my head to say a quick prayer over the meal. I picked up the newspaper and thumbed to the sports section. Susan returned back to the table with a cup of coffee and set it down beside my plate. I looked at her with an appreciative smile. "Thank you." She smiled at me and then went over to the sink to start on the dishes.

After eating my breakfast and reading the paper, I showered and got ready for work. On my way back down the stairs, Susan met me near the front door to open it for me.

"Why are you leaving early?" she asked, her eyes innocent, her face soft.

It broke my heart every time I had to lie to her, so I'd look for ways to modify it. My lies were more comfortable that way. "Just dropping off the extra money I won from the other night."

She smiled. "I can take it for you, dear. I have a list of errands I have to run. I'll just stop by and drop it off in our savings account."

"No!" I accidently snapped from nervousness. "I mean . . . sorry, it's not a big deal. I like the extra commute. It gives me more time to listen to my new audiobook."

"Okay," she replied, a little taken aback. She looked at me and said, "Have a good time at work. See you after your shift."

Relieved that she didn't keep pushing it, I kissed her and told her I loved her. I stepped out onto the porch and thought to myself, *crisis avoided, again*. It seemed that almost every time I withdrew money from the account, I was just a few wrong words or moves away from her discovering my trespasses.

I wanted out of gambling a year ago, but by that time I was already down over half the eighty grand I started with in our savings. Every day at work, every moment I had alone in my days, my mind continuously searched for a way out of the mess I had gotten myself into. The only solution I ever found was winning the money back somehow. On my drive to the bank, I turned off the audiobook I had started and thought about the Vegas proposal the kid had mentioned.

It sounded good, but it was a lot of money.

It would take almost everything I had in my savings. The tournaments I had participated in at the casino were only a grand here and there, nothing that big. Not ten grand!

I made my mind up right there on the spot. Vegas wasn't an option, I wasn't going to do it.

I pushed the thoughts away and turned the volume back up on the audiobook.

Even with the pit stop by the bank, I arrived twenty minutes early to work. I made my way into the multi-purpose room to catch the morning news on the television. I wasn't the least bit surprised when I saw Ted already there, his eyes glued to the TV.

"Hey, Alderman," he said without looking.

"Sherman," I said, taking a seat.

"Did you win?" he asked, again without breaking eye

contact from the television.

"Of course," I replied.

A smile crept from the corner of Ted's mouth as he looked over at me. "You say you win every single time you go up there. If that's true, when you going to say goodbye to being a firefighter?"

I laughed. "I love this job. I'm not going to leave because I won some money. Well, I take that back. I would leave if I won the lottery."

"Whatever," Ted laughed. "You still putting your money on the Mariners for the game this Friday?"

"Yep."

Shaking his head, he replied, "Easy money for me. They suck this year."

"We'll see. I have a good feeling about this one."

"You saw their last game, right?" Ted asked with a raised eyebrow, looking over at me.

"No, but I read about it."

He shook his head. "Huh. Well, you want to put your cash on a team who's not showing up to play the game, that's fine. I'll be showing up to collect."

"We'll see."

Ted and I watched the news until about eight

o'clock. Then we joined everybody as they showed up and headed over to the training room that was adjacent to the dining hall. We had meetings once every two months in there. The meetings were mostly to go over any concerns and to talk about upcoming trainings on-site or out of town. They were usually a pretty cut and dry type of thing. This time it wasn't.

"Thank you all for being here," Chief Paul Jensen said as he stood at the front of the room.

"Like we had a choice in the matter," I said with a grumble.

"Put a lid on it, Alderman. We have some serious stuff to talk about today."

Sitting up a little more in my seat, I leaned forward and asked, "What's going on, Chief?"

Cole walked to the front and stood next to Paul. He looked worried. His arms were crossed and he stood like a nail about to get smacked with a hammer. He wasn't one to be upset over a kinked hose, so it made me worry a little.

Paul crinkled up the paper in his hands and threw it into the waste basket behind him. "I'm not going to read that stupid memo from the Mayor's office. Basically, our station is having part of its budget cut."

"What? Why?" Kane asked.

Brian chimed in. "What's this mean?"

The room was in an uproar. Micah and I were about the only guys keeping quiet. Once everybody settled down, the Chief spoke again.

"Everybody knows the economy has been on a downward slump. We're not immune because we are firefighters."

Grunting a little, I cleared my throat. "Sure doesn't seem to affect the twenty people it takes to stand around a pothole in the middle of the road while one guy fixes it. That Francis Street road project is a joke!"

"Yeah," Kane said, nodding as he looked over at me.

"The city just wasted a ton of money by putting in a splash pad in that new park over on the west side. Why do we get punished for the city's lack of budgeting and responsibility?" Brian added.

"I swear, this city gets dumber by the minute," I said. My words were heavy with grief as I thought about the downward slide the city had been going toward over the last decade or so. Looking up to the front of the room at the Chief, I said, "Paul. Is there anything we can do to stop it?"

Shrugging, he replied, "I'm doing everything I can since I found out. I'm going to meet with some of the city officials to see if there is any possible way around this."

"What exactly are the cuts going to do?" Ted asked the Chief.

"No raise this year for starters. That'll be frozen. Some personal cuts, pensions, that kind of stuff." Everybody started talking at once, so nothing was comprehendible. My worry soared at the mention of pensions. I was only a few years out from retiring. Once the yapping died down again, I looked Paul in the eye. "You'd better fix this."

"We'll figure this out, Alderman," Paul replied, giving me a confirming nod. It helped that he seemed so confident.

Cole unfolded his arms and said, "We protect the people in this city. We suffer, the city suffers. I think we can draw on that fact alone and hopefully get some adjustments made to the budget."

Cole was right. The city officials were aimed toward helping the community, and cutting back on safety wasn't helping anybody. They'd be jeopardizing their own citizens. "Yeah. Maybe they're just unaware," I said.

"I'll keep you all updated and in the loop. Would anyone object to a group prayer?" Cole asked.

There were no objections.

Cole bowed his head, and we all followed suit.

Cole said, "Dear Heavenly Father, we come to your throne with humble hearts today. We are worried about our station and the men that serve this city. Please let your will be done with the matters of the city. Not our will, your own. We pray these things, in your name, Amen."

I liked Cole. He had a good head on his shoulders and was a good fit for the role of captain after Thomas Sherwood passed away. The Chief had approached me first about the open position of captain, but I declined it. It was too much of a headache to deal with all the drama and the guys around the station. I wasn't cut out for caring that much. I just liked showing up and doing my job and then going home.

While the meeting went on for another half hour, I didn't pay much attention. I kept thinking about my pension.

A call came in later that day for a fire. Suiting up in my turnouts, I turned to Cole as he walked behind me on his way to get into the ladder truck. "Hey," I said.

"Yeah?" He replied, stopping and looking at his watch. "Make it quick."

"If you and the Chief have issues getting Mayor Gordon to fix this . . . I say we take it to the streets."

One of Cole's eyebrows shot up as he crossed his arms. He looked slightly confused at my wording.

"What do you mean, Alderman?"

"Door knocking. We can get her fired or something. The community loves us firefighters."

Cole nodded. "We don't need to get her fired, but you think that'd work? To get supporters."

Shrugging, I replied, "It couldn't hurt anything. At least a petition or something. We get a pretty good return for the boot fundraiser thing we do every year."

"Yeah, but that's for children with muscular dystrophy."

"Still, it's us out there. I think it could work."

Cole nodded. "I'll keep that in mind." He climbed up into the truck's front seat.

Getting into the back seat, I looked over at Ted as he sat next to me. "Sherman. Don't you think that we could knock on doors and get people to support us and help stop—"

"Let me stop you right there. I don't think this city cares about anything other than having fun and doing whatever they want. People all over this country have turned a blind eye away from what the government is doing, and they only focus on themselves."

"This isn't political, Sherman," I retorted.

"Yeah it is! Everything is political. Don't you get that? Have you looked at the city budget? We might be getting cut, but the special programs for the down and out are getting a surge."

"Really?" I asked, skeptical.

"Yeah. It's all on the city's website. They put it out there for anyone to read. But like I said, nobody cares about what the government is doing, even on the local level," Ted replied.

As the fire truck rolled out of the bay doors, I shook my head. "What happened to the good old days, Taylor?" I asked, leaning up toward him and Greg in the front.

Cole looked back at me. "They're called *old* for a reason. We'll get it figured out. Don't lose any hair over it, Alderman."

Sitting back in my seat, I looked out my window as we flew down the street toward the fire down on the 1600 block of Garfield. The trees, cars and scenery looked like a smear across my field of vision as I thought about the looming financial troubles between the station and the city.

As we arrived at the scene, jolting me out of my thoughts, I jumped out and headed to the rear of the truck. Pushing up the flap that hid the hose, I grabbed the hose end and my hydrant wrench.

Running down the road with the hose over one shoulder, I arrived at the hydrant. Wrapping the hose around it once, I shot a glance back to the truck to see Ted pulling out the slack from behind for me. I began to twist the end onto the hydrant. After I finished hooking up the line and got the water flowing, I jogged over to the truck to grab my halligan and then to the house where Ted was arranging the hose for the frontal attack on the fire. Flame and smoke danced across the sky like a ballet recital, moving and shaping itself as it went, the smoke almost mirroring the rhythm of the fire. Arriving at Ted's side in front of the house, I asked, "Anyone still inside? Do we know?"

Ted nodded. "Nobody inside, we're all clear."

"Okay. Let's rock this fire." Putting my mask over my face, I walked over and picked up the end of the hose that lay in the grass.

The heat from the flames jumped from the house and warmed me through my jacket. That warmth was comforting, a feeling similar to a second home. In my earlier years at my previous station, the heat had bothered me. It wasn't until I got used to it back about a decade ago that I found the warmth oddly comforting.

While dousing the flames outside the house, I spotted Brian climbing down a ladder from the roof after doing ventilation cuts.

The flames died down on the front side of the house and we were able to advance through the door. Stepping inside, I shoved my halligan up into the ceiling to make sure there was no looseness to it. Soot fell into my face from above. It was okay, so we proceeded. I saw flames in the kitchen to the left, so I directed the nozzle in that direction. Water streamed across the room and into the kitchen as I adjusted the pressure on the nozzle. I placed my left foot back behind me to brace myself as the water roared from the hose. Spraying back and forth across the kitchen in a swath, the smell of wet burned wood and a soon to be victory filled my nostrils.

As we were cleaning up and returning the equipment to their rightful places on the back of the truck, Cole walked over to me.

"Alderman," he said.

"Taylor," I said, not pausing from my task of putting

the hose onto the truck.

"Are you going to come to that men's breakfast tomorrow morning?" he asked. "It's after we get off. At ten," he added. The men's breakfast was a meal that Pines Baptist put on every month to help draw in friends and family that didn't usually participate in church services.

"Sure," I replied. I have felt guilty going to anything outside of Sunday services since my addiction took its full form, but I couldn't come up with a reasonable excuse to not go to this one. "The wife will be out shopping. I think it'll work." I flashed him a forced smile.

"Great," Cole replied. "I'll see you there."

CHAPTER 4

The smell of coffee filled me with joy as I opened the front door the next morning, arriving home after my first twenty-four hour shift for the week. I kicked off my boots in the living room and tossed my jacket onto the couch as I excitedly hurried into the kitchen.

"Good morning, Rick," Susan said from the kitchen table as she read the paper. She had a cup of coffee, her reading glasses and a piece of toast that was half-eaten sitting on a plate.

After pouring my cup of coffee, I joined Susan at the table. Taking a seat, I said, "I have a men's breakfast at Pines Baptist that I'm going to head to in a bit." She smiled warmly at me as she replied, "That's neat, dear." At my nod, she closed the newspaper and handed it across the table to me. Her eyes looked down to a notepad that I presumed was her shopping list. Glancing up, she asked, "Was there anything special you needed at the store?"

"Nope."

"Okay. Have fun at the breakfast, and I will see you later." She ripped the paper from the notepad and folded it in half twice. Getting up, she went to the island in the kitchen and slipped the list into her purse that sat on the counter.

She left the kitchen and went into the living room. I flipped open the paper and found the sports section. I shifted my eyes over to the window beside me as I heard a bird squawk outside. Looking out the nook's window toward the guest house in the backyard, I couldn't see a bird anywhere in sight. Instead, I saw an old walker belonging to Susan's mother leaning against the far eastern side of the house. I recalled her mother living out there during her last days. She stayed with us until she passed. It felt like forever, but it was only for four months. Susan had spent a great deal of time out in that guest house with her mother. The memory of that time dissipated from my mind, losing focus and bringing me back to the reality of the guest house. Brown boxes pushed up against the dirty glass windows inside. Boxes, boxes and more boxes. There were more boxes in that house than any one person should have. It had been six years since her mother died, and since that day the house's only purpose has been an oversized storage unit for Susan's shopping addiction.

"Rick, what did I tell you about these boots? You need to keep them by the doorway!" Susan shouted from the living room.

Turning in my chair to face her, I said, "Why's it matter? They aren't dirty."

With the boots in hand, she hurried her steps across the living room and up to me. She showed me the dirt that was clumped onto the bottom. "I love you, but that's not clean. Some got onto the carpet, Rick!

You know how I hate that."

"Sorry," I replied, turning back to take another drink of my coffee.

The phone suddenly rang on the wall. Susan flashed me another grumpy look and went over to answer it. She set the boots down on the floor in the kitchen and picked up the phone.

"Hello?" she said.

I picked up the newspaper in front of me and began reading the sports section again. After a few moments, Susan turned to me.

"Rick," she said, pulling me away from the paper.

"Yes?"

"Beth wants to know if she and the kids can come down for dinner this evening." Our daughter Beth lived east of Spokane, out in Coeur d'Alene with her husband and our three grandkids.

"Of course," I replied, smiling. Ever since she, Jonathan and the kids moved out to Coeur d'Alene, we hadn't been able to see them as much as we did when they lived in Spokane. Standing up, I left the kitchen and went upstairs to shower.

When I came back down, it was nine thirty and

Susan was still on the phone. Stopping in at the kitchen to look for my keys, I kissed Susan on the cheek. "I gotta get going to that breakfast if I don't want to be late, let Beth know I'm excited to see her. Have you seen my keys?"

She nodded and covered the phone. "Sorry about earlier when I lost my temper. Your keys are over on the counter next to the fridge."

"I understand, I'll be sure to keep them by the door. Love you," I replied, ". . . and thank you." I walked over and grabbed them before I headed out the door to leave.

Pulling into the parking lot of Pines Baptist, I saw Micah and Kane strolling across the pavement, heading toward the front entrance. They weren't aware of my vehicle pulling in, so as I drove past them I honked a little. They both leapt up at least a foot in the air, and Kane shot a look back like he wanted to kill me. Then his face softened into a smile as he saw that it was me.

He waved as I pulled up alongside the both of them. Rolling down my window, I said, "Hey. You here for the free food too?"

Micah grinned. "Good food, good people. Nowhere else I'd rather be this fine morning."

I nodded.

"You back in church, Alderman?" Kane asked.

Shaking my head, I said, "Our pastor was out sick. It's been a few weeks now since I've been."

"Go visit him," Kane added.

I laughed. "I don't want to get sick!" I replied. "At my age, I'm one bad sickness from ending up in a hospital."

"Oh, come on." Micah laughed. "We're not that old. I'm only a couple of years behind you."

"Yeah . . . well, have you gone to seen him?" I asked.

"He's not *my* pastor. I didn't even know he was ill," Micah replied.

Nodding, I looked behind me as a car was waiting for me to move. "I'll see you two in there," I said, rolling my window back up. I spotted Cole up by the entrance of the church as I pulled into a parking spot.

Once inside, I got my plate of food and made my way to the table with the rest of the guys from the station. Sitting down with a mountain of hash browns, four sausages, two strips of bacon and a couple of eggs, I saw Micah give me a funny look. "You're so worried about your health that you won't go see your pastor, but you're eating all that?" he said with one eyebrow lowered.

"Yeah. It doesn't make much sense. But it is what it is." I laughed. Looking over at Kane, I said, "You ever going to start back up with poker night?"

Shaking his head as he finished his bite of toast, he wiped his mouth with a napkin and said, "No. I don't think so, man."

Cole added, "He's pretty busy with his girl, Kristen."

Kane laughed. "That's partially it. But I've also started helping out a ton with the Youth Group at Valley Baptist. Eats up a lot of my time."

Nodding, I replied, "I see."

"Top of the mornin' to ya'll," a man in a white dress shirt and jeans said as he patted Cole's shoulder and greeted our table. I couldn't recall if it was the pastor or not. I hadn't been to Pines all that often. He shook Cole's hand and smiled at the rest of us. "Glad ya could come down for breakfast. We're gonna have a guest speaker here in a few minutes."

"Pastor Holland, Good morning," Cole said. "What's the topic for this morning?"

"Blind faith," he replied, keeping that smile front and center on his face.

One of my eyebrows shot up and the pastor caught it. He looked at me "I see your skepticism, but maybe you'll enjoy it. I don't believe we've met," he said while extending his hand.

"Rick. Rick Alderman," I replied, accepting the handshake.

"Rick. You'll enjoy it." He smiled again. He was smiling so much that I wondered if he ever stopped—even when he went to sleep at night.

Cole nodded at the pastor and then looked over at me. "Blind faith is required time and time again in life. It's a reoccurring theme in all avenues across our lives."

"I agree," Micah said, nodding as he wiped his mouth with his napkin. "Life is often unpredictable, and it's our faith and trust that God is in control that gets us through."

Someone from a nearby table called out to the pastor. He said his goodbyes and went on to the next table. I noticed he kept on smiling as he went. I grunted a little with a laugh as I said, "There ain't nothing blind about my faith." I pointed down at the table, pushing my index finger against it. "I know what I know because I know it's true."

Micah set his fork down and looked at me. He was sitting next to Cole and Kane. "Come on, Alderman. You haven't ever felt your faith and trust was blinded?"

I shook my head. "Maybe in the beginning I was a little blind . . . but I've been in church for thirty-five years; ain't nothing I don't know."

Micah's eyebrows furrowed, but he remained quiet as he picked up his fork and continued eating. Everybody else stayed pretty quiet at the table. The only sound at our table was the sound of our silverware clanking against our plates.

"Those blueberry pancakes were something else, weren't they?" A loud voice on the microphone interrupted my thoughts as we turned to see who was speaking. Standing on the stage was a happy man, seeming even happier to get everyone in the room's attention on him. "They *were* delicious. And now that our tummies are full, I should introduce myself. I'm Jacob Brighton, but my friends call me Jake . . . so you can call me Jake."

Rolling my eyes as I directed my attention back to my plate of food, I continued eating as I listened to him.

"Today I want to talk to you about blind faith. What is blind faith? Faith in the Scriptures isn't blind. It's tested and true. Right?" He held up his Bible for a moment in the air as he turned on one foot, showing it to everyone in the room.

"But I've got a secret to share with you. There's something you might not know." He paused his words to draw the focus of the crowd. I even turned and looked at him. He continued, "A blind faith is not only encouraged, but needed in times of uncertainty. When you woke up this morning, you knew you were coming down to Pines Baptist to eat some breakfast, right? Well, I hope you knew . . . or maybe you're like Jeffery over here, whom I met this morning." He pointed over to a table. "He got a wakeup call from his brother-in-law, asking if he'd like to come along. He didn't wake up knowing he was coming here. But chances are that you did." He walked the stage as he paused again.

He said, "You got in that car, turned the key over and drove down here. Or you got a ride, or whatever way you came today. And that act of coming here took a form of blind faith. Your car didn't break down. You didn't get in a wreck."

Oh jeez, I thought to myself. *This guy is being a bit ridiculous. That's not blind faith.*

"We are putting our faith in *something* whenever we make these countless decisions in life. Blind faith doesn't have to be like Abraham in the Bible when God told him to leave everything he knew to follow him or when asked to sacrifice his son. It can be small or big. For instance,"—he looked back at our table and pointed—"If you're like the guys in the back from the fire department, blind faith is running into a burning building. That's faith and trust in God to protect them. It's blind because you don't know the outcome."

Leaning over my plate, I whispered to Kane, "We train for that, it's not *blind faith*. We trust God to protect us, but we're not blind. I don't like the analogy he's using."

Kane lowered an eyebrow at me and whispered back, "Hush, man. I'm trying to listen."

Leaning back in my seat, I crossed my arms and kicked out my feet beneath the table. My skepticism and coldness was growing for the speaker.

"In the Bible . . ." he began to say. Suddenly my ears perked up. Talk was cheap and easily found, but when someone started talking Scripture, that's when I begin to listen. I had little tolerance for stories like driving a car to communicate a point. With his Bible open, he continued, "In Matthew 9 we find a ruler who is asking Jesus to lay hands on a deceased daughter. Blind faith. In Chapter 9 we also find a woman with such a strong faith that she believes just touching the edge of His garment will heal her. Blind faith."

I knew the stories by heart, but I couldn't help but snicker under my breath a little at the connections this guy was trying to make. It was cute for a twenty-something-year old kid to get up and talk in front of all of us men, but the connection wasn't there in my mind. I could tell he caught my laughter, but he didn't address it on the spot. He continued the talk with us until arriving at his final conclusion.

"I believe *blind faith* will find us all at different points in our lives. Sometimes it's evident, other times not right away." He looked me in the eye, and then he continued his gaze across the room. "Let us pray."

After the prayer and breakfast was over and everyone was getting up from their seats, Jacob approached me.

"Hi . . . ?" he said, extending a hand as he waited for a reply.

"Rick Alderman," I replied, shaking his hand.

Jacob cleared his throat and said, "Hi, Rick. I noticed that you laughed while I was teaching . . . which is fine with me. But, could you explain why? I'm kind of curious."

Shaking my head, I put my hand up and tried to shoo him and the awkward situation I had found myself in away. "No, it's nothing." I tried to leave the table since all my other buddies had already left.

He caught my arm in a non-aggressive way to stop me. "Please?" he asked. "I'm new at this. I can handle constructive criticism well, and it'll help me for the future . . . if you don't mind?"

I pursed my lips together to form a thin line. Then, I looked at my watch. I had a few moments to spare for the young man.

"Okay. Well, those people and stories you referenced . . . I don't think they really had *blind faith*. They already were interacting with Jesus. They were trusting in what they already knew to be true." Jacob raised an eyebrow at me as he nodded slightly. "Do you *feel* that you don't practice blind faith, Rick?"

I shrugged. "I don't think so. I've been a Christian for a long time. I feel like I know what I believe pretty well and that term—blind faith—has always been a bad one from where I come from." I looked over at a couple of guys that were lingering in the back of the room who seemed to be waiting to speak with Jacob. "Ya know, a term for people who don't understand what they believe—following blindly like an idiot." I nodded my head toward the guys in the back. "Looks like you have a couple of guys waiting for you. I'll let you go."

Jacob nodded and turned to look at the gentlemen in the back of the room. "Okay. Well, thank you for indulging me in that. I appreciate it, Rick." He shook my hand again and I left.

CHAPTER 5

Deciding to stop in at my favorite diner—Heidi's—

on the way home from the men's breakfast for
another cup of coffee, I was glad to see my favorite
parking spot was open. I already had java that
morning, but it wasn't about that. It was about good
conversations with good people. The whole crew
knew me well, and the owner and cook, Ron
McCray, was like a father to me. He was the main
reason I had been going there at least once or twice

a week since I was just a lad. He was an older gentleman, in his late seventies now, but one of the wisest men I had ever met in my life. He was practical, down to earth, and the type of guy that would give you the shirt off his back if you needed it. Our relationship went clear back to when I delivered newspapers to the diner as part of my first morning paper route when I was twelve.

Pushing open the glass door, I made my way over to my barstool along the front section of the diner. As I took a seat, Penny, my regular server, came over and flipped my coffee cup right side up and poured me some black coffee.

"Mornin' Ricky," she said, smiling as she popped a bubble with her gum. Penny was about sixty or so—I didn't know her exact age. She had been there at the diner for most of my life, but she moved away ten years ago to Arizona with her husband. Once he passed away, she came back to Spokane, figuring it was the only thing left to do. Never having had a child of her own, she felt aimless in life and even once admitted to me that she came back to die. Luckily, she found a second wind for living when she returned to the diner to serve again. Taking care of the patrons of Heidi's brought her joy and fulfillment in life.

"Mornin' Penny, you're lucky I still let you call me that after all these years," I said, smiling as I took a sip of the steaming hot coffee.

"You'll always be little Ricky to me." She laughed.

"No fires to fight today?" Ron said, smiling as he came through the kitchen's swinging doors. Ron loved being the cook. His skin was almost like leather in the summer months; he'd tan instantly as soon as spring hit, and then he would get darker and darker until winter when his skin would return to a lighter leather look. Ron had wrinkles everywhere, but they were the charming kind of wrinkles that gave the impression that he knew something. For all the pain and heartache he had gone through in his life, I felt inspired every time I talked to him. He seemed happy and cheerful no matter what was going on in his life.

"Nope, no fires today. Plus, they needed a break from me," I replied, grinning. "What you got going on today?" I asked as he ambled over to me and leaned across the bar top.

He shrugged and leaned his weight on both arms as they lay across the bar top. His eyes scanned across the diner, taking in all the people that were there and enjoying his masterpieces that he crafted in the kitchen. "Some of this, some of that. Might take the *Old Girl* for a spin this afternoon."

Ron's *Old Girl*, as he liked to call it, was a 1964 Pontiac GTO that he bought after he and his late wife, Heidi, made their first profitable year at the diner. His wife didn't get more than a few years of enjoying *Old Girl* because she unfortunately passed away. Even though Heidi was gone before I ever met Ron, I knew by the way he talked about her that she was one classy lady.

Glancing over to the windows, I said, "It should be pretty nice out today. Have you taken her out yet this year?"

He nodded as he threw the dirty dish towel over his shoulder. "I did mid-June a couple of times. But outside of that . . . not really. My ability to handle a chill in the air just ain't what it once was."

"I hear ya. I can't be like Elsa either. *The cold bothers*

me in my older age," I replied with a soft smile, knowing he would get the reference because of his grandkids.

He laughed. "I'd love to be as young as you are, Rick!"

"I'm anything but young," I replied, rubbing the corner of my coffee cup with a thumb as I looked down at it.

"Psh. You'll be around for a while, Rick. Don't fret. The good Lord gave you a life; you can't let age control you. God has a plan for your life."

"Well, you agreed when I told you a couple of weeks ago that chief wanted us to write a will," I retorted.

He shook his head, smiling as he looked down for a moment and then back at me. "Well, yeah, ya dummy! A will keeps your stuff in order if something happens to you. I didn't mean you were going to die soon! Did you get 'er done?" Ron asked.

I shrugged. "Wrote a few lines . . . wasn't a very comfortable task."

"Hire someone to write it for you. That's what I did. I told him what I wanted it to say and then signed off on it after I read through it."

Nodding, I looked at him and said, "I could do that." The bell above the diner's front door chimed, and we both glanced over to see who it was. I was without words when I saw that it was the kid from the casino. My shoulder turned sharply away from the entrance in the hopes he couldn't see me.

"Blaze," he said, taking a seat up at the bar next to me.

Just ignore the nickname and maybe he'll leave you alone, I thought to myself. I looked up at Ron and he looked confused.

"Blaze?" Ron asked the kid. "I think you got the wrong guy. I'm Ron."

The kid laughed and shook his head. "Oh. Umm . . . coffee with creamer." I was relieved he didn't direct Ron's attention to me and point out the fact that it's the nickname I went by at the casino. Ron and I didn't talk casino or poker. It wasn't something I ever talked about with him. Ron was a devout Christian and even led the choir in his church up until a couple of years ago.

Ron gave the kid a nod and headed down the line to the coffee pot that sat on the counter behind the serving station.

"What are you doing here?" I spoke quietly.

He laughed. "Came here for some food, what else do people come here for?"

"This is *my* diner."

"You own this joint?" the kid asked, glancing around. "Had no idea you were *that* rich."

"No . . . I mean I've been coming here for a long time. These people are like my family."

He shrugged and shook his head. "Okay. What's the big deal? You don't want me eating here?" he asked as Ron brought his coffee back over to him and set it down.

Ron gave me a weird look. I wasn't sure if he heard anything. Ron left to go back into the kitchen.

"You can eat here. I don't care. It's just strange to see you in here."

"Thanks for the permission." The kid laughed.

"Sorry . . . I didn't mean anything by it. Just weird that you're here."

"It's fine. What you been up to? Playing any more tournaments up at the casino?" he asked.

Leaning in closer to the kid, I lowered my voice as I

responded. "I don't broadcast my poker playing around here."

He returned in a whisper, "Okay. Have you been playing?" he said quietly.

"It's been like what . . . a few days since I've seen you? No. I haven't been back there."

"Well," he said. "Do you want to play some poker?" He turned and looked around to make sure nobody was close enough to hear as he continued. "Check this out. Me and a couple of close friends are getting together tonight for a little game. You know . . . *just the guys*. It's friendly, but it's high stakes."

Intrigued, I asked, "What's the buy-in?"

"$2k buy-in, $50k pot."

"Wow," I replied, leaning back in my seat.

"Yeah," he replied, putting a hand on my shoulder.

"It's going to be sick. You in?"

"Tonight?" I asked as I thought about my daughter, Beth, and the grandkids coming down for a visit.

"Yeah."

"What time?" I asked.

"Five. Probably run until about eight," he replied as he took a drink of his coffee.

I raised an eyebrow. "That's kind of strange. Rather early . . ."

He turned to me and shrugged his shoulders. "So what if it's early? Who cares?" he put a hand on my shoulder and shook it. "It's going to be fun."

"Well, I don't know. My daughter is coming into town. Probably won't work out," I said, taking my coffee and bringing it to my lips.

He nodded. "Family *is* important."

"Yeah."

Penny came over to check on Robert, and he ended up ordering some food.

I stood up to leave. Dropping a five from my wallet onto the bar top, I gave Penny a nod. "Thanks for the coffee. I'll catch you guys later. Tell Ron I said bye."

"Have a good one, Ricky," she said, smiling as she chewed her gum.

Turning to leave, Robert suddenly grabbed my arm and stopped me. Handing me a card, he said, "The address is on the back if you change your mind. Five—sharp."

I took the card from him and glanced at the address.

It was clear down in the valley. Leaving the diner, I slipped the card into my coat pocket and put it out of my mind.

Getting home as Susan was unloading the groceries from the back of the car, I hopped into action and helped her out. I reached into the trunk and grabbed a few sacks. Following her inside, I set the bags down on the counter near the fridge.

"How was the breakfast?" she asked as she set her grocery bags down on the island in the kitchen.

"It went well . . ." My words trailed off and she could see through me.

"What happened?" she asked, pausing from unloading the groceries.

"Got into it a little bit with the guest speaker." My head hung, as I knew how she felt about my little spats with others. For the first five or so years of marriage she tried to correct me on them, but over time she learned it was just part of who I was.

"Rick," she said with a disappointed tone.

"Susan, you don't understand. He was trying to tell us that we have to rely on blind faith in life. I don't find my faith to be blind whatsoever."

She nodded, but only to acknowledge what I said. She didn't say anything, just went back to unloading the groceries. On the way back out to the car to get the last few bags, I followed her, catching up to her side out by the car.

"Do you think we have blind faith, Susan?" I asked.

She shrugged. "To a degree, we all do."

"Hmm . . ." I replied, grabbing the gallons of milk from the trunk.

She nabbed the last plastic bags and shut the trunk. Coming back inside the house and on her way into the kitchen, she said over her shoulder, "Beth called. She won't be able to make it in until eight thirty tonight."

"No dinner tonight with her and the kiddos . . ." I said, opening up the fridge in an attempt to hide my intrigue.

"Yeah. But she'll be here for a few days, so that'll be nice."

Putting the milk into the fridge, I shut the door and

looked over at Susan. "A few days?" I asked, surprised.

"Oh, stop it, Rick. It won't kill you," she said as she dug into the sacks and began putting the rest of the food away.

"I know . . . just seems strange. That's a lot of time off from work. Can she take that much time off from the hospital?" I asked.

Nodding, she replied, "She had vacation time."

"Oh . . . I see." I went around the island and sat down at the kitchen table. Peering out the window at the guest house, I noticed an elliptical machine sitting on the porch. I laughed.

"What's so funny?" Susan asked as she put away the pasta in the pantry.

"You bought an elliptical?"

"On my way out of the neighborhood this morning, I saw a garage sale and stopped. I got that for five bucks, Rick!" As she spoke, her eyes were lit up like a Christmas tree.

Shaking my head, I laughed again. "You buy so many random things that we never use."

Shutting the pantry door, she came over to my side

and joined my gaze across the backyard at the guest house. "It's not random. There are lots of useful things out there. I'm going to use that elliptical."

"We don't use the *stuff*. That's why you wheeled the elliptical to the guest house instead of inside."

"I just put it there for a minute, Rick," Susan said as she pulled her hand away from my shoulder. She went back into the kitchen.

"I was out there looking for my drill bits, and I spotted a few items that are probably from two black Fridays ago that you still haven't ever pulled out and used."

"They'll make easy gifts this year," she defended herself.

"Why didn't they become gifts last year?" I asked.

"Or the year you got them?"

She said nothing.

"Yeah," I said to her empty reply.

She seemed to be done with the bantering and took off down the hallway.

Beth wasn't going to be in until eight thirty.

Suddenly, I had time for that poker game. I pulled the card that had the address on it out from my coat pocket.

The valley.

Off Sprague.

It was far. At least thirty minutes.

But it's fifty thousand bucks. That could get me pretty close to even. Suddenly I heard a door shut and Susan's footsteps returning back down the hallway.

I slid the card back into my pocket.

She turned the corner and came back into the kitchen.

"Hey. I'm going to go play some poker tonight," I said, trying to sound nonchalant as she came over to me at the table.

"Okay. What time is that?" she asked.

"Five."

"With the guys from the station?" she asked.

"Yes," I lied.

"Oh, that's great!" she replied, beaming. "You guys haven't gotten together to play in a while. I'll bet this charity will appreciate it! You should give the money to the homeless shelter down on Division this time. With the holidays around the corner, I bet they'd probably be happy for the extra support!"

I hated lying to her like this. It broke my heart. It was uncomfortable and wrong in so many ways. But I had to keep the lie going or I'd have to explain everything. I couldn't do that. I'd explain it to her someday, but it'd be later, not now.

"I don't know, dear," I said. I stood up and excused myself, heading to the bathroom down the hallway to escape the conversation. She didn't deserve these lies, but I felt trapped.

Once in the bathroom, I shut the door and locked it. My anxiety rose and my chest started to hurt. Placing a hand on each side of the sink, I leaned into the mirror and my reflection. Looking at myself, I didn't like who I saw.

I saw a man who had hidden the truth from his wife for three years. I saw a man who was putting himself first instead of others. I saw a man who was a liar.

I was sick of the lie and the man I had become.

I told myself as I looked into the mirror at the man I did not like, *tonight is it.*

The last time.

The last chance.

Then, it's over.

I just needed to win the fifty thousand that night, and then I'd come clean to Susan. That was only thirty grand short of the eighty I started at three years ago. I knew she'd be upset about it, but these lies weren't going to rule my life anymore.

CHAPTER 6

It was exactly five o'clock when I arrived, with the
sun still high in the sky, but lingering clouds gave off
a dark and shady appearance. There was a chain link
fence with a gate surrounding the lot, with the
warehouse smack dab in the middle. I saw Robert
leaning up against the fence near the entrance. It
almost felt like he was waiting for me, knowing I
wouldn't be able to resist. He opened the gate for
me as I pulled in.

It had rained the hour prior, and I noticed small puddles in spots across the wet pavement in the parking lot. I pulled up beside a midnight blue Porsche and parked. I felt a little uncomfortable with the vibes that the situation was giving off. I didn't know these people. I hardly knew Robert. Frozen in place as I sat in my car, I didn't move. I just sat there, debating if I was doing the right thing.

Knocking on my car door, Robert smiled through the rain streaked window at me. I rolled it down.

"You coming or what?" he asked. He looked at me and then over his shoulder toward the warehouse.

Shaking my head lightly, I said, "I don't know, man. This seems . . . not right."

"It's poker. Maybe you would feel comfortable if you just give me a cut of your money right now? That's the only difference between this and the casino. Or is it something else? You worried about your old woman?"

I thought of Susan. She wouldn't be happy about what I was doing. But then again, she wouldn't be happy about the missing seventy thousand out of the bank. I had to do this. End it once and for all.

I shook the thought from my head, took a deep breath and got out of my car.

"Let's do this," Robert said. He patted my shoulder and let out a chuckle as we walked to the entrance of the huge warehouse. The exterior was smooth aluminum, giving off a newer look—all except for the door, which was old and rusted.

Once at the door, the kid turned to face me and lifted a fist to knock. A couple of firm pounds of his fist and he let his hand fall back to his side. He tipped his chin at me and said, "You ready for some real poker?"

I gave him a nod, but I didn't say anything.

Opening the door, a bearded giant of a man answered. While his face was covered in a dark and thick patch of wool, his head was bare. His eyebrows were long and looked to have plans of their own as they went in a few random directions. His appearance unsettled me, and I felt my anxiety percolate.

In a deep and smooth voice, the large man said, "Who dis?" He looked over at me. His eyes were as dark as his beard.

"This is Blaze. He's with me," the kid said, patting the giant's chest with the back of his hand. He strolled by him without an ounce of fear.

"Nice to meet you," I said, following after the kid. The giant remained quiet and furrowed his eyebrows as I walked past him. We heard the door slam shut behind us as we kept walking.

"Bobby!" A man with a cigar between his teeth shouted from a table that sat in the open and dark warehouse. The warehouse was relatively dim as the only light source hung down above the poker table. The man smiled as he rose up and pulled the cigar from his teeth. He had a ridiculously tiny mustache. His hair was black as the night's sky, and it was combed over to one side. He wore a gray, pinstriped suit and a pair of white shoes. He stood with open arms toward Robert, just barely in the edge of the light.

There were four other guys at the table that looked over at us as we approached, but there were no introductions for them.

"Lincoln," Robert said with a gracious nod as he took off his leather jacket and laid it across the back of one of the empty chairs that sat at the table. "This is Blaze, or Rick Alderman, the firefighter I was telling you about."

"Ahh, I see. Welcome, my friend," Lincoln said as he sat back down and picked up his cigar, eying me.

"Thanks for having me," I replied, taking a seat next to Robert. I pulled out my wallet to get the money for the buy-in.

Lincoln laughed a little as he shook his hand at me. "No . . . don't do that. We make it right at the end, yes, my friend?"

Looking around the table, I felt a jolt of uneasiness settle into me. Standing up, I said, "I forgot that my daughter is coming into town tonight. I gotta get home."

"I understand," Lincoln replied, nodding slowly. "I have kids myself."

Lincoln took a puff of his cigar and blew the smoke out of his nostrils as he shook his head. "Have a good night, but it is a shame. The way Bobby talks about you, it seemed like you're pretty good. I was looking forward to playing."

I looked over at Lincoln. "Okay, I'll play." I sat back

down in my seat.

"I understand your nervousness, Rick. I would be too, coming down to a warehouse to play some poker."

"Yeah." I laughed. "Little odd."

He smiled. "Let's play." He looked over at the guy with the deck of cards and said, "Go ahead and deal them out, Frankie."

Frankie shuffled the cards a couple of times and then began dealing. After the dealing was done, he grabbed stacks of chips and pushed them across the table to me.

"Thanks," I replied.

Frankie said nothing; he just sat back down.

Picking up the corners of my cards, I saw that I had a two of hearts and a nine of clubs. I folded.

Glancing past one of the other guy's shoulder, I saw giant cloth blankets faintly in the dark, draped over something in the distance.

Lincoln looked over to see what I was looking at, and then he looked back at me. "You curious what's under those covers?"

Shaking my head, I said, "No." I started to worry

until Lincoln broke out in laughter.

"Bear," Lincoln called over the man from the door I came in at. Bear came over to his side. "Pull the covers off for our friend. He's lookin' a bit nervous still."

Bear glared at me and then walked over to the blankets. He pulled them off to reveal pallets and pallets of diapers.

Lincoln took a puff of his cigar as he grinned at me. "I buy and sell diapers, my friend."

Relieved at the sight of the innocent diaper boxes, I smiled. My imagination made me think it was drugs or weapons or something crazy like you see in the movies. My nerves settled, and I felt my anxiousness fade away.

Lincoln, Robert, the others and I played poker for the next couple of hours. I felt all the more comfortable with every minute that ticked by. Lincoln told me about a trip down to Cancun he and his wife had just went on last week and about his daughter, Emalia's, latest hobby of collecting rocks that she found around the yard. He seemed like a relatively normal guy. The fact that my chip stacks were growing quite nicely through the evening was also adding to my easygoing feeling. Each time I beat someone off the table and took all their chips away, my confidence swelled, and I could see winning the fifty grand within my sights.

By the eight o'clock hour, it was just down to Lincoln, the kid and myself. Frankie dealt the cards out to us as Lincoln lit up another cigar from his metallic cigar holder that he had sitting next to his bottle of whiskey.

I glanced at my cards. Ace of diamonds, king of diamonds. My face stayed stone cold and emotionless as I was bursting inside with excitement. I relaxed the cards back onto the table and waited for my turn.

I raised to four hundred.

The kid kept his usual one earbud in as he stayed stone-faced, debating somewhere in his mind what to do, I suspected. My eyes went to his chips. He had about two grand worth of chips left in his stacks. It wasn't much compared to Lincoln's or mine. The kid called.

It was now up to Lincoln, who seemed to be busy on

his phone while he waited for his turn. He paused and looked at the table for a minute. There weren't any cards down, just the ones in front of him that he had failed to even look at yet.

"How much?" he asked, looking at the both of us.

"Four," I said.

"Thousand?" he asked.

I looked at the pot. "Hundred."

"Okay." He grabbed for his chips.

"You haven't looked at your cards, though. Don't you care what you have?" I asked.

He shrugged. "It will be okay." He tossed in his chips to match and continued to do whatever he was doing on his phone.

Shaking my head a little, I thought to myself, *this is easy money*. I had hardly been there for three hours, and I was already almost done wiping the table clean.

The pot was good and Frankie burned a card. Then, he turned the flop. Three cards.

Ace of hearts, king of hearts and a two of hearts.

If my internal emotions had a set of external speakers, I couldn't ever play poker. I was jumping up and down inside with excitement. On the outside, I kept my cool and raised the pot by a thousand dollars in chips.

The kid rubbed his chin as he removed an earbud. "Blaze . . ." he said, shaking his head. "Why you gotta kill me like this?" he laughed.

I said nothing.

"Screw it." He shoved in the rest of his chips, which raised me another six hundred on top of mine.

Lincoln looked over at the cards from the flop and set his cellphone down. He looked to be a little more concerned now that there were a couple of grand on the table. Glancing at his cards, he laughed and then looked over at me. "Rick. You married?"

I nodded.

"Your wife ever get on to you about forgetting to take out the trash?" he asked, setting his cards back down on the table.

"Of course," I replied.

"My wife is texting me to inform me that I haven't taken the trash out in three days, and she's looked every day to see if I would take it out, but I haven't." I laughed. "My wife can be cute like that too."

"When's your garbage day? Mine falls on Monday, and it just agitates me like no other. Monday is already a busy day."

"Thursday is our garbage day," I replied. Realizing he was taking a short break from the game to chat, I relaxed in my seat and turned my attention to him. He nodded in acknowledgement. "You know what I wonder? Why not take it out yourself or at least let me know about it? Why trap me like that?" Lincoln said, shrugging as he looked over at the kid.

"I know how that can be. I've been married to Susan for over thirty years, and we still seem to get into it once in a while. You'd think after a while you just wouldn't have anything to argue about anymore." Suddenly, Lincoln took his stack of chips and matched the kid's raise and then raised it another grand.

Looking at the cards on the table, I wondered what he could have. It had to be a bluff; he didn't even look at his cards before the flop. I raised his bet—this time, ten grand.

Robert was already all-in and said, "Woah . . . looks like things are heating up."

I smiled over at him. "Don't have all night, right?"

Lincoln called my bet without hesitation.

The turn card came—two of diamonds.

It was up to me. The two did nothing for me, but I had to play my two pair. I raised it another grand.

He doubled it.

I tripled it.

He called. "Feeling confident, Mr. Alderman?" he asked.

Shrugging, I laughed. "Been rockin' it so far. Just hoping to ride the wave."

Frankie flipped the river card over: it was an ace.

Secured the full house. Three aces and two kings.

Glancing at my watch, I saw it was already almost nine now. I bet the same amount, only a grand.

It was up to Lincoln. He raised it to fifteen thousand.

Got him.

Pushing all my chips in, I said, "All-in."

Lincoln grinned. "Flip 'em."

"You calling?" I asked.

He nodded softly as he tossed out a pair of pocket twos. "Four of a kind," he said. My mouth fell open.

Robert flipped over his cards, a queen and a king.

And I flipped over my ace and king.

"It was nice playing with you, *Blaze*," Lincoln said as he stood up from his chair and reached across the table to shake my hand.

Shaking off the shock, I stood up and nodded. "That was a solid win, Mr. ?" I said, shaking his hand.

"Lincoln's fine, my friend," he replied, smiling as he took his cigar and put it out in his ashtray. "You can pay Bear on your way out. I assume you brought cash?"

Nodding, I said, "Yes. And okay. Thanks for letting me come."

Leaving the table, the kid followed right behind me. He patted my shoulder. "You were so close, man!" He began walking backward with a jump in his step.

Coming up to the door to leave, I pulled out my wallet. "Here you go," I said, handing Bear the two grand in the form of hundreds.

He counted it out in front of me and then stopped. "Where's the rest?" Bear asked.

"What?" I said. "That's all of it. Should be two thousand there." I leaned over his hands that held the money.

"It was twenty thousand," he replied coldly.

A knot the size of a baseball twisted inside my chest as my anxiety came rushing back like a wave crashing up on a beach. "What do you mean?" I said with a shaken voice.

The kid pushed my shoulder. "Twenty G's, just like I said."

"You said two," I replied sternly back to the kid.

"Yo, Link! We got a problem," Bear shouted over my shoulder across the room to Lincoln. His voice bounced around the room, finally reaching Lincoln. The knot twisted harder.

In a loud whisper, I said to Bear, "Hey . . . Robert said two thousand! What is this? I don't have that kind of money." Lincoln walked over to us from the table.

"What's the problem?" Lincoln asked, looking at all three of us.

"Bobby's friend here doesn't have your money." He growled under his breath my direction, setting my heart off in pounding that I couldn't stop.

Lincoln pulled his head back and scoffed. "What? I'm sure Bobby's friend can get it to us tomorrow, right?" Lincoln asked, looking over at me.

Shaking my head, I said, "I don't have that kind of money lying around."

"You told Bobby here that you were debating on Vegas. That's a ten thousand dollar buy-in. Obviously a man of your caliber can afford twenty grand."

Shaking my head, I said, "Robert . . . um . . ." I furrowed my eyebrows at the kid as my heart beat harder. Then I exploded in frustration. "This kid lied to me! He told me it was two grand! Not twenty!"

"Bobby, is this true?" Lincoln asked, shooting a deadly look over at Robert.

"It was twenty," the kid replied, lying.

Lincoln looked back at me with a lowered eyebrow. "You thought you were going to sit down and have a chance at fifty grand with a two thousand buy-in?"

"I thought there were more than a few people playing when I heard it. Then when I got here, the thought never crossed my mind."

Lincoln laughed as he raised a hand out to me and shook his head. "No. Don't try to play me for a fool. Make it right, Rick. You're a man of honor." Lincoln slid his hands in his pockets and walked away without another word. On his way across the smooth cement floor of the warehouse, he stopped and looked back. He said, "Drop it off in the mail slot of the door you came in by tomorrow night at six." He turned and continued his stroll across the floor.

Bear had hardly opened the door before I darted out and across the parking lot to my car. My heart pounded in my chest as sweat beaded on my forehead. I struggled to hold my key steady enough to unlock my door.

"Blaze!" Robert shouted, startling me from across the parking lot.

I steadied my hand enough to get the key in the hole and unlock the door. I quickly got inside my car and started it. The kid was just outside my car window now. "What do you want?!" I shouted through the still rolled down window. "Just leave me alone, kid!"

"Dude, I'm sorry; I didn't realize I told you two. It was twenty."

I rolled up the window and shouted, "YOU make it right then!" Backing out of the spot next to the

Porsche, I sped over to the gate and waited for the kid. He came over and opened it. Not even giving him a look, I peeled out of the parking lot and back toward my side of town.

CHAPTER 7

After getting out of the Valley, I pulled into a grocery store parking lot to catch my breath. Still trembling as I turned off the car, I pulled down the visor and looked at myself in the mirror. I had never been through anything like that before in my life. I was terrified. Suddenly, I heard a honk behind me. With a quick jerk of my body in the seat, I turned around. I was relieved to see it was just a couple of cars honking at each other in the parking lot.

"Get yourself together, man," I said out loud, slapping the visor back up against the roof. Flinging the car door open, I stepped out and took a deep breath of the cool night air. Taking another deep breath, I felt my nerves empty themselves out onto the wet pavement below. Leaning over the back end of my car, I yakked again. I wiped the brim of my mouth and stood upright, relaxing my back against the trunk for stability.

Suddenly, I let out a laugh.

"He sells diapers . . ." I said. Turning myself over on the trunk, I pushed myself fully upright with my hands. My nerves settled.

Shaking my head, I felt myself return to a state of normalcy—well, as normal as I could feel right then. I got back into my car and put it all behind me. My daughter and wife were at home with the grandkids. I needed to focus on that. Not some diaper guy from the Valley. Pulling out of the grocery store parking lot, I left feeling a lot better than when I'd arrived.

Back at home, I was greeted by two of my daughter's three children. Natalie was seven years old. She ran up and wrapped her arms around my leg as she smiled up at me.

"Grandpa!" she shouted.

Philip, the three-year-old, came running also, and he latched onto my other leg. "Grampa!" he shouted up at me.

Smiling down at both of them while I patted their heads, I said, "I missed you two so much!" I lifted my eyes up to my daughter, Beth. "I wish every time I came home I could have this kind of greeting."

She laughed a little as she came down the hallway to join us near the front door. "Hi, Dad." Her smile was warm and beamed with joy as she put her arms around me. She was such a happy woman. Even if her husband was working a ton back in Coeur d'Alene, she never complained about it.

"Where's little Gregory?" I asked.

"He fell asleep on the couch waiting for you," Susan replied with a bit of an undertone to her voice.

I nodded, but I didn't say anything.

"Game went pretty late?" Susan asked as I picked up

the grandkids from my legs and brought them into my arms.

"Yeah. Almost won," I replied, walking down the hallway past her.

"Funny . . . because Cole called asking to talk to you," Susan retorted with a sharp and accusing tone. My gut turned at her words. She caught me right in the act. My mind raced from idea to idea, trying to find a lie. "That's odd. Kane invited him along with the others to come. Kinda wondered why he wasn't there." After I said it, I knew it didn't make any sense and that she was on to me. Making my way into the kitchen, I set the kids on the floor and got drink cups for them.

As I handed them each a cup of water, Susan cut into me from over near the island. "He acted like he knew nothing about it," she said, trying to be quiet.

"Hmmm . . ." I replied. Looking over at Beth, I asked, "How was the drive in? Hit a lot of traffic on the way?" I hoped Susan would drop it.

Beth shook her head. "It wasn't too horrible. There was one wreck though that looked pretty bad. A semi-truck full of bees fell over into a ditch, bees loose everywhere. It was a mess."

"Oh jeez, did you see it happen?" I asked, looking at her across the counter as she stood next to Susan

Out of the corner of my eye, I could see Susan's gaze fixated on me. If steam could come off the top of her head, it would have right then. I could sense it and I avoided looking at her.

"No. They just had cones out and tons of police as I drove by. I searched the radio after I passed the scene to find out more about the wreck, and that's when I heard it was a truck full of bees."

"Huh. Strange. Jonathan wasn't able to get the time off this time?"

"No, they're short staffed right now; it was pretty short notice, anyway," she replied.

"Grandpa. Could we go to the mall?" Natalie asked as she wrapped an arm around me after dumping her cup into the sink.

"It's too late for that," Beth said as she looked at the stove's clock. "In fact, let's get you two into bed." Philip began crying as he reluctantly walked over to his mother with his arms out for her to pick him up.

"Aww," I said, tilting my head as I watched him.

"Don't let his cute face fool you," Beth said as she took him up into her arms and grabbed onto Natalie's hand. She led them out of the kitchen and down the hallway toward the spare room.

I smiled as I watched them walk down the hallway. Susan came over to me. I tried to make an escape by turning to leave the room, but she stopped me.

"Rick," she said sharply.

"Yeah?" I replied, looking over at her.

"Where were you?" she asked. She sounded more concerned than angry.

"Playing poker," I replied.

"Don't lie to me, Rick. We've been married far too long for these games," she replied, leaning a hand on the counter as she tilted her head and looked at me.

"It was poker, Susan." I took a breath in and let go as I continued. "But it was with some guys I know . . . not the station guys, but other ones. A guy from the casino invited me to it."

"Why did you lie to me?" she asked, lifting her hand off the counter and taking a step closer to me.

Taking a step back, I said, "Why do I have to explain myself all the time?"

"This is a marriage. You can't be untruthful to me . . ." She paused for a moment. "This is unlike you, Rick." She came closer and touched my arm. "Are you okay? Are you going through something like . . . a midlife crisis? You can tell me. That's what I'm here for."

Pulling my arm back, I said, "Stop it, Susan! This is why I didn't say anything. It turns into something bigger than it is. Just drop it, please." Seeing Beth come down the hallway out of the corner of my eye, I raised my eyebrows toward the hall to try to stop Susan from talking about the poker anymore.

"Did they go down okay?" I asked, side-stepping away from Susan.

"Yeah," she said, coming into the kitchen. She rested her arms onto the counter and let out a big breath. "Natalie's been such a handful lately . . . starting to get a real mouth on her."

Susan came over to Beth and put an arm around her. "She's getting to that age. I remember it like it was yesterday with you. You started paying more attention to your hair and listening to the radio." Standing up, Beth smiled over at Susan. "Yeah.

Instead of radio, it's YouTube and an obsession with my phone and—she's so mouthy!"

"You gained quite the little mouth on you, too. Maybe it's payback," I said, trying to keep the mood light.

Susan said, "Just nip it in the bud before that habit turns into a problem. A problem is when you have a teenager with a mouth!" Shaking her head, Susan said, "You were such a handful!"

"Thanks, Mom." She proceeded past Susan and into the living room to scoop Gregory up into her arms. "I wish they could just stay this young forever," she said to us as she stood at the couch with him in her arms and a soft smile on her face.

"You want them to stay two? I hated that age—no offense," I said, coming into the living room as she held him in her arms.

"Yeah. But they're still just babies when they're two . . . still willing to cuddle a whole bunch and be babied." She left the living room and headed down the hallway to the spare room.

Susan came into the living room and right up to my face. It annoyed me. "You'd better not make lying to me a habit, mister!" She pushed her index finger into my chest, driving my agitation through the roof. Who did she think she was talking to?

Laughing under my breath, I glanced past her out the window toward the guest house. "Yeah, just like you don't make shopping a habit."

"Don't you dare! You know I used shopping as a therapy mechanism after my mother passed away. I have a budget and I stick to it. Bills are paid. I never lie to you about purchases either! Don't compare it to this! We go away to the casino twice a month. That should be enough."

Her words cut through me. The casino getaways were good for us, but they weren't enough for me. I had to keep doing more. I looked at the floor and sighed. "I don't want to talk about this anymore. I'm getting tired."

"Because I'm right," she replied righteously.

Standing there for only a moment longer, she turned and walked into the kitchen.

Leaving the living room, I headed to the stairs to make the climb up to bed.

"Going to bed, Dad?" Beth asked, stopping at the

base of the stairs when I was about to reach the top. I smiled and looked back at her. "Yeah. It's been a long day. I'll see you in the morning if you're up."

"I have a two-and-three-year-old that are up at six every morning. I'm sure I'll see you." She jogged up the stairs to meet me halfway. Her arms wrapped around me. "I love you, Daddy."

"I love you too, dear," I replied before giving her a soft kiss on the cheek. My mistakes in life were plenty, but Beth was a huge reminder that I've done something right.

Releasing from our embrace, I continued to the bedroom and settled underneath the covers. Looking over at the picture of my wife that sat next to my Bible on my nightstand, I felt a slight twinge of sadness creep over me. She was so hurt by the little she knew; if she ever found out the truth, it wouldn't just end us—it might just break her.

After saying my prayers, I reached over to the lamp and turned it off. Rolling over, I thought to myself, *I have got to find a way to make this right.*

CHAPTER 8

My eyes opened to something I didn't see too

often in my lifetime: my wife sound asleep beside

me. Slipping out of the covers, I snuck out of the

room and down the hallway to the bathroom, being

careful not to make too much of a ruckus. As I got

into the bathroom and shut the door, I looked at the

mirror that hung above the sink. I looked old.

Walking over to the countertop, I leaned a hand on

each side of the sink and raised my chin to look at

each side of my face. Gray was starting to show itself through the stubble that was coming in. I shaved. "Where did all the time go?" I asked myself as I toweled off my face and looked at my aging reflection in the mirror.

Coming out of the bathroom and down the stairs, I saw Beth getting the two boys up into their boosters at the table. Greg was yapping his mouth a hundred miles an hour as I came into the kitchen. Most of the words he was saying were incomprehensible, but it was cute nonetheless.

"Is that right?" I asked him, smiling. I walked over and poured a cup of coffee from the freshly brewed pot. Looking over at Beth, I said, "Thanks for putting on coffee."

She looked back at me and said, "I didn't."

Looking back at the coffee pot, I recalled the timer feature.

I knew it was Susan.

A smile came across my face. Even though she was angry, she still made sure my needs were met. It warmed my soul and gave me comfort to know she still cared.

"Wanna go drink a cup of coffee in the back once I finish getting these kiddos some cereal?" Beth asked as she pulled out two bowls from the cupboard.

"Yeah." Looking at my watch, I said, "I have a few." Heading out the white French glass doors that led out onto the deck, I stepped outside and into the backyard. Taking in a deep breath of the morning air, I took a seat in one of the mesh patio chairs we had set around the dark bluish-gray table.

My eyes surveyed the yard beyond the deck and stopped on the guest house. All it took for me that day to not feel so bad for Susan was to take one look at that guest house. Shaking my head, I said, "She has some nerve buying all that and getting upset about a poker game."

"What?" Beth asked, stepping out from the open door and down to the patio chairs. Taking a seat, she kept her eyes fixated on me.

"What, what?" I replied, trying to deflect.

"It sounded like you were talking out here, but I couldn't hear you from inside," Beth said.

I shook my head.

"Where is Mom? I've never seen her sleep in . . .

wait. Are you two fighting?"

Shaking my head without delay, I said, "No."

She took a drink of her coffee and set it down on the table. "You don't have to lie to me. I'm twenty-eight and have been married for a while now."

I laughed. "It doesn't really matter, it's okay. Promise." Raising an eyebrow, I shifted the conversation. "How is everything going in Coeur d'Alene?"

Nodding softly but steadily, she said, "Its going good. The kids love their school, and Jonathan and I love our new church family. It's a good change."

"Happy to hear," I replied.

She scooted closer to the table and took another drink of her coffee. Setting her cup back down, she nodded again and said, "It really is. I know you worried about us not being as close, but we're still *pretty close*, Dad. I have a friend, Cindy. Her parents and family all live in New York . . . that's some *real* distance!"

Smiling, I replied, "I'm glad you didn't move that far away, but I still worry about you."

"You don't have to worry about me, Dad. We're

good."

"You're my daughter. I'll always worry about you," I said.

She smiled as she looked out into the yard. "You and Mom going to church again yet? She said something a week or two ago about the pastor being sick?"

"We will." Looking at my watch, I saw I was running a few minutes behind. Getting up too fast, I felt a slight twinge of pain in my back. "Ah," I let out a painful moan for a split second.

"You okay?" Beth asked, concerned.

"I'm fine . . . just getting old." Standing upright, I turned to one side and then the other to stretch. The pain started to dissipate. "I'd better get going. Have a good day with Mom. I'll see you tomorrow morning."

She stood up and hugged me. "Don't ever die, Dad."

"Don't talk like that. I'm young. Still have quite a bit of time left."

She smiled at me as we released from our embrace. Going inside, I saw Natalie coming down the hallway with her blanket in one hand. She looked half asleep as she slowly made her way across the hardwood floors.

"Morning, Princess," I said to her as I stopped for a moment.

"Morning," she replied, rubbing one of her eyes. "Where you going?"

"I'm off to work," I replied. Walking over to her, I kissed her forehead. "I'll see you tomorrow."

"Okay," she replied. Looking at her mother, she asked, "Do they have cinnamon toast here?"

"Yeah, we do," I said.

A smile came across her face as she continued over to the table. "I want that, Mommy," she said, looking at Beth.

I went over and kissed the boys goodbye before heading out the door to the station.

Walking into the multi-purpose room, the guys were all sitting around the TV like flies hovering around a cow's tail.

"What's going on?" I asked, walking up to the group.

"Shh," Ted said from the couch, trying to quiet me.

"It's the Mayor. She's having a press conference."

"Oh," I replied. "What's she saying?"

"Stop talking and listen," Kane snapped.

Looking at the TV, I saw Mayor Janice Gordon talking to a group of reporters. She was standing behind a wooden podium and she looked frazzled, judging by the constant shaking head she seemed to have going.

"Like I have said from the beginning of all this: If parts of the city don't like something, let's talk. My door is always open, and if you have a better idea, I'm all ears."

The cameras went off, snapping a million or so pictures within the span of a few seconds. Then a bunch of reporters' hands went up in the air. She pointed to one in the front.

"Yes, in the blue tie."

"Hi. From the Spokesman Review, we want to know why the funding for the people who serve the community is being cut while you leave programs in place such as the study of bacteria in the Spokane River that's still fully funded."

I laughed. "Like to see what she says about that," I

said, crossing my arms.

"I had no idea about that. See, the problem is that I can't possibly know *every* single thing that's going on in this city. Spokane is big, and I have no way of knowing exactly where all the money is going all at one time. I did what I thought was best, but I will leave my door open for those who want to reach out. Thank you." She stepped away from the podium.

Cole stood up and turned off the TV manually. He said, "You heard her, the door is open. I say we go knock on that door and help her do her job."

"Well. We can't really just walk up to her door, so how do we go about that?" Kane asked.

"I liked Alderman's idea of canvassing." Cole looked over at me. "We can get people to rally for it. Let's start with a petition and get a good rally going in front of city hall. We'll come knocking on that door all right." Cole looked over at Ted. "Sherman, could you collect data on what we all do here as far as fires per year and all that good stuff? We need to show how we need to keep things the same with our station."

"Got it," Ted replied.

"Good." Looking at me, Cole said, "Alderman, I need you to figure out a game plan for canvassing. Are we going to stick to our neighborhood? Or is this going to be city-wide with more stations involved?"

Kane raised his hand and Cole looked over to him. Kane looked at all of us as he said, "We have hose training today."

Cole sighed. "Oh, yeah. Forgot about that." He thought for a moment and then said, "Work on this stuff when you can. We aren't going to get everything done in one day. I'll go talk to Chief Jensen about our plans."

Everyone nodded in agreement.

Cole took off out of the room and everyone began to get up and get busy. Micah looked at me and asked, "You doing all right? You look a little worried."

"I'm fine," I replied.

Brian jokingly knocked me in the arm with his elbow. "He's just getting old. Probably needs a nap or something."

I laughed. Rookie was getting better with his humor. "I'll need a nap after laughing my butt off today watching you try to tackle a hose again."

"Pshh . . . it's cake. I've done it before," Brian replied. "Last time was pretty entertaining, Rookie. You chased that hose around the parking lot for at least three minutes straight."

"Well, I'm ready this time," Brian said with a confident tone as he left the multi-purpose room.

All of us made our way to the training grounds around the back of the fire station after lunch that day, which was basically just an over-sized parking lot. It had a burned up cement building in the back corner, a couple of fire hydrants, and lots of smooth pavement. There was also a small shop-like structure that sat toward the back of the lot, right in front of one of the fire hydrants. That's where we all met, fully suited up in our turnouts.

Cole walked up from across the pavement and smiled at us all. "You boys ready for some hose training?"

"Depends. Rookie might not be so ready," I said.

Cole shook his head. "We're not doing solo hose

drills today. We'll be focusing on group exercises."

My eyebrows shot up. "That's a bummer. What kind of hose and pressure are we doing?"

"Two and a half-inch hose, and a hundred fifteen PSI," Cole replied.

I looked over at Brian. "That means 'pounds per square inch,' Rookie." I smiled jokingly.

"Shut up!" he snarled.

"Sounds fun," I said to Cole. "We going to make it a little interesting and get that PSI up to one-fifty?"

"We'll see how one fifteen works out. Gomer will take lead first."

Brian nodded, but he looked a little nervous under that helmet. Stepping up to his side, I patted his shoulder. "It'll be good. Just be careful with the nozzle. It gets a little crazy at those higher PSIs."

"Okay."

"Alderman, go hook up the hose and get it ready," Cole instructed.

"All right," I replied. Jogging lightly over to the truck across the pavement with Micah, I saw a car sitting up near the road next to the firehouse. Stopping, I covered my eyes to get a better look, but then it took off down the road. Brushing it off as paranoia, I continued onward to the truck.

Cole, Micah and I had a barrel of laughs as we watched Brian, Kane, Ted and Greg all wrestle the hose for the next couple of hours. Getting up from the hose after I clamped the water off, Kane came over to the three of us.

"How about you old men try?" he asked, panting heavily as he took off his helmet. The water and sweat mixed together as it almost poured off his head.

We all three looked at each other and shrugged. Cole gave Kane the clipboard he was holding.

"I'm down," Cole said. Looking over at me, He said, "Let's show these boys how it's done."

Nodding, I told Kane, "C'mon, man the hose clamp, McCormick."

Brian and the rest came and stood by Kane as Micah, Cole and I circled around the hose. I smiled up at them as we waited.

"Child's play," I said with a hearty laugh. "It'll be like the good ol' days, like that fire down on Division at the old Mill shop."

Micah laughed. "Man . . . that hose was out of control. I thought it was going to kill someone."

"Yeah. We got lucky. You guys ready?" I asked.

They both gave me a confirming nod.

Shooting a look back at Kane, I said, "Let 'er rip!"

Kane loosened the clamp, and the water came gushing through the hose line and out of the end of the nozzle. Cole dove for the hose first, but it whipped itself out of the way before he could grab onto it securely. Pacing my feet back and forth as I tried to line up for it, water shot up into the air as the nozzle's end launched upward and twirled.

"Come on!" I shouted as I danced with the hose. Micah dove onto the hose way down the line. Then I went for a closer spot up near Cole as he was scrambling.

Got it.

Using all my strength, I grabbed on to it and held my position as I knew Cole was about to jump back on. Cole latched on right behind me and helped gain control. Micah's help on the back end secured our positioning on the hose. We got control quicker than the other guys did by a long shot. Kane reclamped the water.

"Wow . . . I'm impressed," Kane said, approaching us with a long clap.

Smiling as I pushed myself up off the cement to rise to my feet, I said, "It's called teamwork."

Cole said as he stood up, "We know how to work together extremely well. You can't try to be a hotshot and win it all. It takes all of you at once— which we seem to have to remind you all every time. There is no *I* in team."

Kane nodded. "I guess I was trying to be *the one* when I was jumping right at the nozzle each time."

"Yeah," Micah said as he stepped up beside Cole. "It seems like a good idea, but without someone having your back, things are going to get messy and you'll lose control."

"That's why we started having a group hose training," I said. "Don't beat yourself too hard, McCormick."

"I'll try not to," Kane laughed. "We haven't really done these much in the past. I'm glad we're going to start doing these more often."

Around the dinner table in the dining hall that evening, we all sat waiting anxiously for Micah's firehouse specialty—Chicken Alfredo. The smell of the French bread cooking in the oven filled the air as my mouth watered.

"About done in there, Freeman?" Cole called out, leaning back in his seat in an attempt to get a better look into the kitchen.

Micah popped his head out of the kitchen doorway for a moment. "It's getting there." He smiled and vanished back into the kitchen.

"Man, I love this meal," Brian said, glancing back at the kitchen for a moment and then folding his hands together in front of him on the table. "My Widow Maker burgers might be good, but his Alfredo . . . Mmm. I bet I could eat that stuff every single day for the rest of my life and I'd be happy."

"Maybe the taste wouldn't bother you, but it'd mess your body up. He puts cubes of butter and loads of cream cheese into that Alfredo sauce! That's why it's darn tasty. Healthy? No way," I said.

Cole raised an eyebrow at me as he cocked his head to one side. "When did you get health conscious, Alderman?"

I shrugged. "I'm not health conscious, but something like this every day would wreak havoc on anybody's body. That's just logic."

"Yeah, it's definitely not an 'eat everyday' type of meal, that's for sure," Cole replied.

Micah brought in a big vat of the Chicken Alfredo and set it down on the table. Steam rose up from the pot as he took off the lid and set the pot holders down next to it and returned to the kitchen to grab a second one. He made plenty, knowing how much we all loved this dish.

"Let's bless the food," he said, setting the second pot down and bowing his head. "Cole?"

"God, Thank you. Thank you for our station, our brotherhood and this meal. May you please bless Freeman's hands that prepared it and bless this time we are about to spend together."

Everyone said, "Amen."

"Dig in," Micah said.

"Need bowls and forks," Ted added, getting up from

his chair.

"Oh, yeah," Micah said, laughing.

"I'll grab them," Ted said, following Micah into the kitchen.

"You were saying earlier that your daughter is in town," Cole said from across the table, looking at me. "How are the grandkids doing? Been a while since you've seen them, right?"

"Yeah. It's been a while. They're doing well from the little time I've seen them so far."

"I talked to Chief Jensen earlier. He said you can take an extra couple of days off."

"I don't feel it's necessary. Thanks, though."

Cole nodded. "No problem."

Micah returned with the French bread in hand. Following behind him was Ted with the forks and bowls. We all began serving up our bowls as we heard the bay doorbell buzz downstairs.

Everyone looked around at each other, wondering if someone was expected. "Anyone know who that might be?" Cole asked.

Everyone said, "No."

"Rookie," I said as I grabbed the spoon and dished

up my bowl.

Brian set his fork down and let out a sigh. "Fine . . ." he said, standing up from his seat as he hung his head and headed for the stairs that led down to the door.

"Man, I hated being the rookie back in the day," Kane said, laughing as he watched Brian leave the room.

"Everyone's a rookie at some point," I said. "They tormented me. Some of the stuff they pulled . . ." I shook my head. "We'd be fired if we did it nowadays."

"Like lighting your sheets on fire?" Cole asked, grinning.

I laughed. "Yep. Exactly. Taylor knows the story. Man that was ridiculous, not to mention dangerous!"

"Really? That happened?" Ted asked as he took a bite out of his piece of bread.

"Yep," I replied. "They had a fire extinguisher so it wasn't that big of a deal—"

"Alderman," Brian said from the doorway of the dining hall.

"Yeah?" I asked, turning to him.

"There's some guy here for you downstairs."

"Some guy?" I asked, partially nervous that it was the kid from the poker night. *How'd he know I was here! At this fire station particularly?* I wondered. I felt a mixture of anger and nervousness.

"Yeah. He said that he's here to talk to you." Brian came back over to the table and sat down.

"Okay," I said. Cole had known me too long not to notice my nerves about it.

"I'll come with you," Cole offered, standing up from his seat.

"No. That's okay. I got it," I replied, holding up a hand to Cole. There was no way I'd drag Cole into this mess. I got up from my seat and proceeded out of the dining hall and down the stairs to the bay. Getting to the door, I took a deep breath and placed my hand on the doorknob. I opened it up.

It was Ron, from Heidi's diner.

"Ron?" I asked, looking outside and down both ways of the sidewalk outside the door. My nerves settled.

"Sorry to stop in like this, but I had a heavy heart."

Looking over my shoulder, I saw Cole up at the top

of the stairs. Stepping outside, I shut the door behind me. "What's going on?" I asked, crossing my arms.

"Heard you talking to that guy in the diner the other day."

"Yeah?" I replied.

"The kid rubbed me the wrong kind of way. I'm not here to tell you how to spend your money or free time, but I wanted to tell you something ain't right 'bout him."

I wanted to tell him right then, but I couldn't. He'd be flaming mad at me for getting involved in the first place. It was too embarrassing to reveal what happened. "Okay," I retorted.

"You already did . . . it's all over your face." Ron let out a sigh and shook his head. "You're in trouble, aren't you?"

"I'm fine," I replied, adjusting my footing.

"Well, you know where you can find me if you need anything. Can I pray with you?"

I nodded.

Ron stepped closer and put a hand on my shoulder and we bowed our heads. He said, "God. You are our

God, our salvation and our Savior. The world's Savior. It's through your grace that we are standing here today. Help us love you, honor you and always walk in the Spirit. Help Rick with his struggle right now, whatever that may be. And I pray these things in your Heavenly and gracious name, Amen."

"Thank you," I replied, setting my hand on the doorknob behind me to go back in.

"Sorry to bother you at work." He turned and headed back to his GTO that was parked along the curb.

"It's all right. Have a good night," I said with a short wave as he got into his car.

Going back into the fire station, I shut the door behind me. I was happy to see that Cole wasn't looming over me waiting at the top of the stairs. As I climbed the stairs back up to the dining hall, I couldn't help but smile knowing I had a friend like Ron in my life. He wasn't like the other friends in my life that had come and gone; he was one of those few rare gems that you kept around for a lifetime. And I appreciated it. Outside of the station men, Ron was the only true friend I had.

Up in Smoke

CHAPTER 9

The next day I arrived home at eight thirty in the

morning. I found my grandchildren and daughter in

almost the exact same position I had left them in the

previous day.

"Morning, Dad," Beth said as I walked through the

living room and into the kitchen. She was sitting at

the kitchen table holding her cup of coffee with both

hands as the boys were eating their cereal.

"Morning, Beth," I said, smiling as I kissed the side

of her head. I sat down at the table and looked at her.

"How was your time with Mother?" I inquired.

"It was okay," she replied. Taking a sip of her coffee, she set it down and forced a smile. "I miss Jonathan."

"When are you planning on heading back?" I asked.

"This afternoon," Beth replied. "I need to get the house cleaned up and ready for our visitors."

Raising an eyebrow, I asked, "Oh yeah? I thought you were staying longer."

"Jonathan's mother, Julie, decided to come stay with us . . . so I'm going to use my extra time off to clean up." She shook her head as she got lost in a thought for a moment. Then she looked over at me. "She's so critical. If the house isn't spotless, she just gets all upset."

Stretching a hand across the table, I rested it on top of Beth's and said, "My mom was the exact same way with your mother."

"Grandma was like that?" Beth asked, her eyes wide.

"Yep. Even when she was getting older and had that bad hip, she'd zoom around the house and clean during random points of her visit. The bad part about that hip was that she'd sit on the couch and whine after doing all the work she found around the house. I don't think she ever meant any offense, it was just what she was good at . . . and she was trying to be helpful, ya know?"

Beth let out a deep sigh and said, "Yeah. I suppose."

Beth looked up at me with all seriousness as something must have entered her mind. "Is your back still bothering you?"

"What do you mean?" I asked, confused by the question.

"Yesterday, you let out a little sound of anguish when you were leaving for work."

Shaking my head, I said, "I'm just getting older, Beth. Nothing is wrong. Things just randomly ache and hurt."

"I don't want to get old," she said, looking out the window next to the table.

Smiling warmly at her, I said, "Nobody really does."

Susan appeared from the hallway with a full basket of clothing on her hip. Even when she was mad with me, she still lit up a room whenever she entered it. I watched as she walked through the kitchen and toward the living room. She glanced at me for a moment but continued on her way. No emotion, no words, nothing.

"Mom?" Beth said. "What was that? Why are you being so cold to Dad?"

"Winter's not for another couple of months, dear," I said sarcastically.

Susan loudly set the laundry hamper down on the couch and began pulling out clothes, folding them ferociously. "Your father thinks it's okay to lie to me, Beth."

"Susan!" I said, standing up. "Don't drag her into this. She doesn't need to know everything that goes on between us."

Susan threw down the shirt she had been folding and came into the kitchen furiously, heading in my direction. "Why, Rick? You don't want your perfect image distorted in your daughter's eyes? She should know you're a liar!"

My blood boiled at her words. She always *assumed* Beth liked me more than she liked her. "Susan. This isn't the time."

Shaking her head, she scoffed and said, "When is a

good time for you? You never want to talk about anything you don't like! And now I don't know if you're telling the truth whenever we do talk! Do you realize how much that hurts? Not being able to trust the man you've been with all your life, the man who *is* your life?"

"Susan!" I said. "Stop."

She said nothing in reply, just turned and stormed back into the living room to continue folding the clothes.

"Uh. What's going on, Dad? Mom seems pretty upset. What did you lie about?" Beth asked cautiously.

"Don't worry about it, Beth. Unless you want me asking you about every time you and Jonathan get into a spat, leave it be," I said firmly.

Looking toward the living room, I spoke a little louder so my words would carry, "I'm going out canvassing with the guys from the station."

"Okay . . ." Susan replied with a senseless shrug.

"Why the tone?" I asked sharply.

"How am I supposed to believe you, Rick? Anything you say? Plus Beth leaves soon and you're just taking off again. Don't you even care to spend some time with the grandkids?" Susan asked.

"I'm going to get the boys dressed," Beth said, sounding a little wary of being involved in another spat between us. She grabbed both boys and retreated back to the spare room down the hall, where Natalie was still sleeping.

Hearing the door shut, Susan came over to me in the kitchen. "Rick, I love you, but I can't trust you."

"Because I played poker?" I asked defensively.

"You lied to me, Rick. Lied to my face without even feeling a little bad! Do you know how stupid I felt when Cole called?" Susan shook her head. "I was mortified. You're fifty-three years old. You don't need to sneak around me like a child!"

I was ashamed, far more than she could comprehend in the moment. She had no idea of what I had really done, only the tip of the mountain. Fear gnawed at my insides as I contemplated telling her everything right there in that moment. I couldn't bring myself to do it. I was too weak.

"Well, I won't play poker anymore. No casino, no games around town. No nothing."

"I wish I could believe you. I hope that's true," Susan said.

"I am going canvassing with the guys, though."

"What's it for?" she asked. I hadn't told her about the drama with the city and the budget cuts. I didn't want to worry her when nothing was solid yet. It wasn't worth the pain.

"Supporting the local firefighters. Just a petition and rally that the station is doing to draw support from the community," I said. It wasn't a total lie, but it was still shying away from the truth about the cutbacks at the station.

"All right," she replied. "When is that?"

"Not until three."

She smiled and said, "That's good. You get to spend at least *some* time with Beth and the kids before they leave. Jonathan's mother is coming into town . . . ugh."

"Yeah. I heard. I told her my mom was like that." Susan lifted an eyebrow. She looked surprised. "You did?" The corner of her lip curled up in a smile. "I thought you'd never admit that."

"I always knew it, Susan." I smiled at her.

Beth came down the hallway and said, "We should all go to the zoo in a little bit. It'd be fun."

Susan looked over at me with hopeful eyes. It was the least I could do for her.

After the zoo trip, Susan, Beth and I were visiting out on the back deck at the house. The kids were running out their energy before the drive back to Coeur d'Alene.

"Thanks for the fun day today, guys. It was nice having us all together," Beth said.

"Yeah," I replied, beaming as I watched Gregory chase Natalie in the yard just beyond the deck. "The kids seemed to really enjoy it."

Beth nodded. "They were surprisingly good."

"They're always good," Susan added.

Beth laughed. "Sure, Mom."

Suddenly Gregory tripped in the yard and began crying. Susan and I stood up as Beth rushed down the steps and into the yard.

"Come here, my baby," she said, pulling him up into

her arms.

"Is he all right?" I asked from the deck.

Beth pulled him from her shoulder and did a once-over. "Seems okay.

A light knock came from the French doors behind us. Looking over my shoulder, I saw that it was Cole. "Hey," I said, opening the door for him.

He stepped out. "Sorry, nobody was answering the front door, and I figured it was okay to walk in."

Shaking my head, I said, "It's all right, Taylor. You can walk in anytime you wish, you know that." Patting his shoulder, I said, "You get those flyers printed out?"

"Yep." He handed me the stack. "All two hundred and fifty." His voice was a bit skeptical sounding.

"I know what you're thinking, but I think we can get some supporters to hand out extra ones."

"Maybe," he replied. He shifted his sights to the back yard and saw Beth. Walking over to the railing of the deck, Cole leaned over and said, "Long time, no see, stranger. How you been?"

"Pretty good, Cole. Yourself?" she said, smiling as she set Greg back down to play.

"Doing well. Don't you love that age?" he asked, smiling as he watched Greg chase after Natalie in the yard.

She came back over to the deck. "It's interesting, that's for sure."

He nodded. "Megan and I went to Silverwood, that big water and theme park, last weekend. Wow! That was an interesting experience with a couple of toddlers."

"I could imagine," Beth replied.

"It was painful in spots, but we had a good time," Cole said.

Beth came back over to the table and looked at her phone. "We'd better get going if we want to beat rush hour." Turning to the kids in the yard, she said, "Let's go, kids."

The kids began whining and crying as they hung their heads and headed for the deck.

"Why do we have to go?" Natalie asked as she came up the steps.

"Your father misses us, dear, and Grandma is coming to visit," Beth replied.

"Tell them to just come here!" she pleaded.

"Maybe another time," Beth said, scooping up the boys in her arms.

We all journeyed to the front of the house and out to the vehicles in the driveway.

"Drive safely," I said, giving Beth a final hug next to her car. "Tell Jonathan I said 'hi.' "

"I will," she replied, smiling.

My daughter and the kids started on their journey back home. Once her taillights rounded the corner of our block, Cole and I got in his car and headed out to start canvassing.

Coming up on the first street, Oakview Drive, a smile broke across my face. While my feet were aching thinking about all of the walking ahead, I couldn't help but enjoy the arching overgrown trees that created a tunnel down the street. Glancing over at Cole, I saw his awe as he looked up at the tops of the trees.

"That's amazing," Cole said, looking up as we rounded a sidewalk and walked up the street.

"How's everything with Susan going?" Cole asked.

Shrugging, I said, "She's all right."

Cole looked over at me. "I know that tone. What's

up?"

Shaking my head, I said, "You know I like to play poker, right?"

"Yeah."

"Well, I told her I was playing with the guys from the station, and I obviously wasn't. She figured it out because you called that night."

"Oh, jeez. I'm sorry. I didn't mean to cause problems."

"No," I replied, shaking my head. "It's not your fault."

"Yeah. You shouldn't have lied."

Stopping, I looked at Cole. "I shouldn't have to explain myself to her all the time."

Cole didn't say anything.

"What?" I asked. "You think I should?"

"It's marriage. I think it's an obligation you have. To be forthright and honest with your spouse. It's like when we're in a fire, man. You gotta know someone has your back."

"I've worked too long and served my family and community for too many years to get to this point and still explain my every move to someone."

Cole turned and we continued walking. "I don't know, man. Have you prayed about it?" he asked.

"Some. But not a whole lot. I don't know what God can really do about Susan.

"It starts with you, not Susan," Cole replied.

"I've been around for a while, Taylor. I appreciate what you're trying to do, but I'm doing okay. Really." Cole went silent again and just gave me a nod as he directed his sights onward.

Walking up to the first house on the block, Cole gave it a firm knock and held out his clipboard in front of him.

The door cracked open and a young woman with a baby on her hip looked at us. "What?" she asked, keeping the door partially closed.

Cole said, "We're from fire station 9 and we are out collecting signatures."

She opened the door more. "For what?"

Clearing my throat, I said, "The city is trying to cut our funding and it's going to hurt the station. We want to show the Mayor that the citizens are more interested in fire and safety than they are for say . . . the study of bacteria in the Spokane River."

She nodded. "We need you guys. You do amazing work. I'll sign it." She set her baby down in a baby swing inside her living room and signed the petition.

"Thank you," I said as she signed.

Cole nodded. "We appreciate the support."

"No problem," she replied, handing the clipboard back to Cole.

"Here's a flyer, we're having a rally down at the Mayor's office at the end of September," Cole said, handing her a flyer.

She said, "Okay," as she looked at it. "So in a month. I'll try to show up. Why so long until the rally?"

"We need to canvas a good chunk of the city," I said.

"Okay. Can you guys call and remind me or something?" she asked.

"We have your email, so we can shoot you an email," Cole said.

"Do you want more than one flyer?" I asked, grabbing a couple more from my own stack. "You can give them to your friends and family."

"That's okay," she replied. "One is fine. I'll let everyone know though. Like I said before, we need you guys!" The baby began to get fussy in the swing behind her and she said, "Thanks for coming by. I'll see you guys later!"

"Thank you, Ma'am," Cole said. "We'll also post updates on the social media page, so find us there."

She nodded.

Turning around as the door shut, we both nodded to each other. "This is going to work out great," Cole said.

"If we find more people like that, I agree," I replied as he got back onto the sidewalk.

After we wrapped up with canvassing for the day, our stomachs were growling with hunger.

"Let's go to that diner you like," Cole said as we got into his car.

Thinking of Heidi's diner, I worried that the kid might show up. I didn't want to risk a run-in with him. I spotted a gas station on the corner opposite of the street we were parked on. I could go call on my cellphone to Heidi's and see if the kid was there.

"Sure, let me take a leak." I shot a finger at the

corner. "Just stop at that gas station."

"Okay," Cole replied.

"Thanks."

Walking into the restroom and into a stall, I called the diner. Penny answered.

"Heidi's diner, Penny speaking."

"Hey, it's me, Rick. Remember that kid that was talking to me the other day?" I asked.

"Yeah. What about him?" she asked.

"Has he been around there anymore since then? Like today or something?"

"No. Why? What kind of trouble did you get into, Ricky?" she asked, able to see right through my words and hear the concern in my voice.

I sighed with relief. "No trouble. Thanks, Penny."

Coming out of the bathroom, I saw that Cole was in the gas station picking out some gum. Walking down the aisle to him, I said, "Let's go."

"I'm excited. The way you rave about their food, I figure I'm overdue to have a meal there."

"It's delicious. I've tried to get you to go a few times," I replied. "Been going there for a long, long time."

Cole nodded and headed up to the counter to buy

his gum.

We arrived at Heidi's and took a booth over against the west side of the restaurant. Mirrors lined the entire diner with various vintage attire hung above them. Albums, old lunch boxes and random license plates from various states were just a few of the items that filled the walls.

"Pretty neat décor in here," Cole said as he looked around.

"They put that stuff there so you don't get bored while you wait for your food," I replied.

"Hey, now. We aren't that slow at service, ya jerk!" Penny said with a smile as she came up to our table.

I laughed. "It's okay to be slow when you deliver deliciousness."

She smiled again. "What can I get you boys started with?"

"Water," Cole said.

"I'll take a Cola with a squirt of cherry," I said.

"Alrighty," she said, leaving our table.

Cole leaned across the table. "Man, I was not looking forward to canvassing, but I really enjoyed it."

"I did too. So many people support us—it's nice to

know that. Well, the ones who answered their doors seemed to support us."

Cole replied, "Yeah. We don't usually get a lot of thanks in this line of work . . . kind of nice to hear it while hitting the streets."

"Yes it is." Picking up the menu, I searched for the two options I knew I'd not be able to decide on until the last second.

The chicken Parmesan or the broccoli cheddar soup. Those were my favorite dishes at Heidi's, but I could never decide on which one to go for until the last moment. Bringing our drinks over to the table, Penny set them down and pulled out her notepad. "What'll it be?"

"Just a second," Cole said as he kept looking at his menu. Penny looked over at me.

"I'll take the broccoli cheddar," I said, handing her the menu.

"Oh, hey," Penny said, pointing her pen toward me. "Ron said the kid you were with earlier this week came by this morning, but he just looked in and then left. Wondered if you knew anything about that."

Cole shot an eyebrow up. "What?" he asked.

"Nothing," I said, shaking my head in a series of short little bursts. My anxiety began to rise at the thought of Robert looking for me.

"Did you find something you want?" she asked Cole, trying to shift the conversation as she realized I was trying to keep the kid off the radar with Cole.

"Umm . . ." he said, looking back at the menu. "I'll go with the turkey club." He handed her the menu.

"I'll get that right out to you guys," she said, leaving the table again.

"What *kid* is she talking about?" Cole asked, leaning across the table.

"A kid I played poker with. No biggie."

Cole sat back in his seat as he kept his eyes locked on me. "Why'd she bring it up?"

Shrugging, I picked up my cola and took a drink. "I don't know, man. How's preschool at the church going for Bradley?" I asked.

He looked concerned but could tell I wasn't going to talk about it. "It's good. He's having a lot of fun. Megan's been going in and volunteering in the class some too. She seems to be really enjoying all that time around a bunch of kids."

"Well, that's neat," I replied. "We had Beth in preschool at our church from K3 all the way until first grade. She enjoyed it."

"It's nice to get that Christian influence on them through school," Cole said.

"It sure is. How is Megan's mom doing since her husband passed? I always mean to ask, but I don't want to draw attention at the fire house about it."

"Good. She started teaching a crochet class down at Spokane Community College. She does that a couple of times a week. Seems to be keeping herself busy."

Shaking my head, I said, "That's amazing. I always wonder about her when I think about Sherwood."

"She's been through a lot, but she's been piecing her new life together since it happened. Seems like it was just yesterday when the topic comes up . . . a lot of pain still there." Cole hung his head.

"Yeah. Can't believe it's been two years now," I said.

"I still think about that day," Cole said. "Maybe I could have saved him if I did something different— moved a little quicker, been a little more healed up . . . maybe I could have pulled that beam up."

"Don't go there, man," I said. "You did everything you could."

"Yeah," Cole said with a nod. "I can't help but wonder, though."

After our dinner, I went to grab my wallet from the back of my pants and realized I had pulled it out and put it in Cole's glove box.

"I'll be right back, need to grab my wallet."

"I got you," Cole said.

"No, that's okay," I insisted. Standing up, he handed me the keys and I headed out to the car.

Climbing into the driver seat, I leaned over the console between the seats, opened the glove box, and grabbed my wallet. As I climbed backward out of the seat, I was startled.

"Rick!" a man's voice shouted from behind me. Jumping, I bumped my head against the doorframe.

"Ouch!" I shouted as I turned to see that it was Kane. Pushing him in the shoulder, I said, "What are you doing here, McCormick? Why'd you call me Rick, were you trying to freak me out?"

Laughing, he replied, "Cole said you guys were eating here and I decided to stop by and try to catch

you two before you left. Man, you were so scared!"
He began laughing harder, grabbing his stomach as
he threw his head back.

"Funny," I replied with a grunt. Kane was innocent.
He had no idea how paranoid I was that day. "Let's
go back in," I said, locking Cole's car up and shutting
the door. We went back inside the diner to join
Cole.

CHAPTER 10

Four weeks came and went without a peep from

Robert or that shady Lincoln character. It was

nearing the end of September and I was beginning

to think that summer night of poker was just a bad

nightmare. I kept my promise to Susan and hadn't

played any poker since then, and I even began

building my savings back up by selling off some of

my baseball cards and various items from the guest

house that I knew Susan had forgotten about.

Everything seemed to be going okay until the day of the rally out in the park in front of City Hall. I had set out that morning to stop by the bank and fill up the tank before going to meet with the rest of the guys at the station to head over to the rally.

"Good morning, Mr. Alderman," the teller said from behind the counter at the bank. I stopped in to make another deposit into the savings account before heading over to the station to meet up with the guys for the rally.

"Morning, Sally," I replied as I laid the cash out on the counter. I sold my 1988 Best Platinum San Bernardino Spirit Ken Griffey Jr. Rookie card, which went for nine hundred dollars at auction last weekend.

She took the cash and ran it through the little machine she had sitting next to the computer.

"You going to be at the rally today?" I asked.

"For what?" she replied, perplexed.

"The firefighters. You haven't heard about it?"

"Oh, yeah . . . My mom was telling me about that the other day. She said it's at like one this afternoon, right?" she replied as she typed something into the computer.

"Yeah. And we're trying to get the mayor to change her mind about slashing the budget of the fire stations in Spokane."

She shook her head. "That's not cool. We need you guys."

"That's how the majority of people feel, it seems like. I think we'll send the message loud and clear today," I replied.

A receipt printed out and she tore it off. Handing it to me, she asked, "Anything else I can do for you?"

"Not today," I replied, taking the receipt from her.

"Hope to see you there."

Leaving the bank, I walked down the front steps and went over to my car. As I got in, I heard someone from across the parking lot. "Blaze," the voice said loudly. It was a male voice.

Turning as I stood up at my open car door, I saw that it was the kid. I flashed him a nod and got into my car. My heart began pounding so loudly that I could feel it in my ears. I turned the key over. As I was backing out of the parking spot, he jogged up to my car and knocked on my driver's side window. I made eye contact with him for a split second, then put the car in drive and sped out of the parking lot. I wasn't very far down the street when my gas light came on. Pulling over into a gas station parking lot, I glanced over my shoulder at least a half dozen times. I was worried that the kid was tailing me.

Pulling up to the gas pump, I got out and slid my card through the card reader, checking over my shoulder several more times. The pump beeped and I started fueling up. Nervously, I kept my eyes down the road toward the bank. My pulse started soaring as I thought about all that had happened that night four weeks ago. I thought I was in the clear, but I wasn't.

The kid had found me.

"Now, that's no way to treat a friend," the kid said from behind me, in the other direction. I jumped as I turned to him.

"I don't want any trouble," I said, shifting my footing to a defensive stance.

He brought his hands out to each side and said, "You told me to take care of that debt. So I did some things. I'm not exactly proud of these *things*. But . . .

I took care of it."

The gas pump clicked as it finished, startling me.

"Calm down, Blaze . . . or whatever it is you go by these days. Don't ever see you on the tables up at the casino anymore."

I took my receipt from the gas pump and headed for the driver's side door. The kid hastened his steps over to the car and pushed the door shut.

"What do you want?" I asked, looking at him.

"I took care of your debt, and this how you repay me?" he asked sharply.

My eyes fell to his waist as I spotted a gun. "I appreciate what you did, But I got to get going."

"You said to take care of it, and I did." He spat on the ground. "Now it's time for you to repay. You've had plenty of time."

"I don't have that kind of money. That's the whole reason I didn't pay to begin with. That and the fact I didn't know it was that high of a buy-in."

"How much you got?" he asked, tipping his chin.

Shaking my head, I said, "Not much."

The kid stepped closer to me and put a hand on my shoulder. He looked behind him for a moment and then shifted his step even closer. He drove his fist into my stomach, catching me off guard. Pain ripped through my torso.

"Wrong answer," he said, shaking his fist. "Ouch . . . I didn't know that'd hurt."

I wasn't able to stand. He grabbed my shoulder and yanked me upwards, pushing me up against the car.

"How much do you want?" I pushed out as I caught my breath.

"You made me mad, Blaze. I was going to give you a break, but now I want all of it."

"Okay. Let's go back to the bank and I'll get it out."

Shaking his head, he said, "No. Cameras and security guards. I'd rather not go back to prison. How about you drop it off at this address?" He slipped a card in my coat pocket. "Drop it off by noon." He patted my shoulder and said, "Don't try anything cute."

"Okay," I squeezed out as I still hurt. Turning, I grabbed for my door and crawled into the driver seat. I sighed and started to regain my composure. My door was still open.

"Oh, and hey, Rick," the kid said suddenly, leaning down into my driver's side door.

I looked over and up at him.

"I'd hate to see that firefighter rally get *ugly* . . . so really, don't try anything."

He vanished away from my car door and I put my hand on my chest to help myself cool down from the anger. "Ugh!" I moaned as I reached out and smacked the steering wheel.

I drove back to the bank and went inside. Upset and distraught, I returned to the same teller and requested to withdraw all the money from the account.

"Are you okay?" she asked, looking at my head, which was doused in sweat.

There wasn't a farther place I could be from *okay* in that moment, which she could obviously see in my face, but I couldn't say anything. She'd be suspicious. "I'm fine."

"Okay . . ." She began counting out the hundreds in front of me and my heart pounded harder with each bill as she laid it down. Being forced to drain my bank account? What kind of idiot does he think I am? I wondered. He's just a kid!

"You know what?" I said. "Stop. Forget this. Put it all

back. I changed my mind."

"Okay . . ." She began to reverse the process and put all the money back into the drawer.

"We done here?" I asked.

"Yeah. Unless you wanted to do something else. Sir, are you sure you're okay?"

I patted the counter and shook my head. "We're done."

Leaving the bank, I immediately made my way down to Heidi's diner to talk to Ron. He would know what to do to resolve this issue. Some twenty-something year old punk wasn't going to dictate my life. Being pressured and bullied into doing something wasn't something Ron ever tolerated. There was one time when I came into the diner in tears as a young school boy because of a bully I'd had a run in with at school. Ron sat me down on the stool and asked me what happened. When I told him, he shook his head, tossed the towel over his shoulder, and looked me square in the eye. He explained to me why people bully and how I could use my intelligence to battle against the bullies. At the ripe age of twelve, he taught me how to defend myself with words and intelligence, destroying my enemies with intellect. Getting to the diner, I went straight for the kitchen. Pushing open the swinging kitchen doors, I looked Ron in the eyes and said, "Can we talk?"

He nodded.

Penny tapped my shoulder as she was standing right next to me, just outside the kitchen. "Ricky, you know you can't be behind the counter," she said.

"Sorry," I replied, letting go of the doors. "I'll be in that booth over there, waiting for Ron."

"Want some coffee while you wait?" she asked.

"No thanks. It'll be quick."

Going over to the booth, I took a seat. My foot nervously shook as I waited for him to come out. My insides felt like they were boiling with frustration. Ron came out from the kitchen, and I jumped up from the booth to greet him. He shook my hand and took a seat across the table.

"What's the matter?" he asked.

"How do you know something is wrong?"

He shrugged. "I've known you for a long time, kid. You have never come into the back like that. What's up?"

"I got myself in a sticky situation, and I need your help."

"What kind of stickiness are we talkin'?"

"Really sticky."

I explained to him everything that had happened with the poker night and today. He listened and waited until the very end to speak.

"Well . . . there's only one solution, Rick."

"And?" I leaned in closer. "What is it?"

He stood up from the booth and said, "I'll be right back." He took off through the kitchen and disappeared for a few minutes. I didn't know what he was doing, but I was sure he had a masterful and clever plan.

Coming back over to the booth, he sat down and said quietly, "Under the table."

"What?"

"Take it."

Reaching under the table, I felt for what he was giving me, and when the cold metal touched against the palm of my hand, I knew exactly what it was.

Taking it, I pulled it into my lap.

It was a gun.

"Really? What am I going to do with this?" I asked in a loud whisper as I leaned against the table.

"You shoot, ya dummy!"

"You taught me to use my words and intelligence when dealing with bullies."

He laughed heartily. "That was school . . . this is real life. You are being threatened. You have to protect yourself!"

"I don't know if I can shoot someone," I said.

He looked over to see a woman glance over at us. "Keep your voice down," he said in a whisper. "You probably won't have to use it, but if you need to, you'll be glad you have it. I would never recommend killing a person, but you have to keep yourself and those you care about protected."

Looking down at the gun, I asked, "I haven't shot a lot of guns—"

"That's a 22—not a lot of kick, but it'll get the job done. It has a loaded clip with good bullets, so you don't have to do anything other than switch the safety off, cock it and then blast the fool away."

"Okay." I put the gun into my coat pocket and looked at him. "Man, I thought this was over. It had been weeks."

Ron nodded. "I wonder what he meant about doing things he wasn't proud of doing."

Shrugging, I replied, "I don't know. I'm worried about the rally."

"Well, I'd tell the cops there about the threat," Ron said.

"It'd get back around to the station, and I don't want them finding out about all this."

"Well, depending on how bad this guy is, it could be bad, Rick."

Shaking my head, I said, "He's a kid. I don't think it'll get too crazy."

"True. The gun should scare him if he tries messin' with you again." Ron glanced over his shoulder back toward the kitchen. "Orders are lining up for me. I better get back at it."

I stood up from the booth and shook his hand. "Thanks for everything, Ron."

"No problem. You take care and let me know how everything turns out."

"Thanks," I replied.

Leaving the diner, it was about eleven o'clock in the

morning. There wasn't much time to get home, have lunch and shower before meeting up with the guys at the station at twelve thirty.

CHAPTER 11

Arriving at the station, I made it there just as Cole,

Micah, Kane and Brian were getting into Cole's SUV.
I parked and jumped in with them.

Closing the door, I sat back and said, "Thanks for
waiting."

"No problem. This is *your* rally, Alderman," Cole
said.

"Yeah. This whole thing was genius on your part,"
Micah added.

"I don't know about genius, but thanks anyway," I replied, buckling my seat belt.

Kane looked at me with a strange look on his face as he looked at my side. Glancing at where my gun was, he said, "What's in your pocket?"

"Nothing," I replied.

Kane grabbed at my pocket and felt. His eyes widened and his jaw dropped. "That's a gun! Alderman has a gun!"

Cole shot a quick look back at me, "Why do you have a gun?"

"Protection. Why else?"

"You haven't ever carried a gun," Brian said.

"How would you know, Rookie?" I snapped. "You don't know me."

"Hey, now," Micah said. "I know you. And I haven't ever seen you carry."

"Well, I am now. We're all firemen. We know firsthand how crazy life can get. Can we just drop it?"

"Yes, that's true, but none of us have ever packed. Anyway, I agree, let's drop it," Micah replied.

An awkward silence filled the air for a moment

before Cole broke it. "So this rally is suspected to pull around thirty thousand people from around the Spokane area."

"Wow . . . that's a lot of people," Brian said.

"Did we get word on if the Mayor is going to speak?" I asked, leaning up toward Micah and Cole in the front seat.

"They said she'll probably step out and greet the crowd since it's not a protest, just a showing of support for those who protect and serve the community."

"It *is* a protest, though," I replied.

Cole shrugged. "Guess they aren't seeing it that way in her office."

"Man, I sure hope this works," Brian said. "I don't want to get axed."

"You would be the one to get axed," I said. "I'm sure you can go back to flipping burgers or something real nice like that."

"Don't be rude," Kane said. "Gomer has been here for a while, it's time to relax on the blows I'd say."

I scoffed. "Look at you, McCormick. Getting a soft spot for the rookie. That girl getting to you, or do you just remember the feeling of being a rookie? I'm leaning toward that girl's sweet cakes messin' with your head."

"Shut it. Kristen isn't the girl that worked in the bakery. You're mis-remembering, ya old timer."

"Hey now," Micah said, turning to us from the front passenger seat. "I'm about the same age as Alderman."

"Sorry," Kane said, dipping his chin.

"I was just playing with Gomer anyway. He knows I like him."

As we pulled up to city hall, we saw the guys we all chipped in to hire setting up the stage and microphone out on the grass that sat across the street in the park.

"You nervous about speaking, Cole?" I asked.

He shook his head as he shot a look back at me.

"Jensen is doing it now."

"Oh, yeah? I thought you were."

"Nah . . . he thought it was best if it came from him."

"I see," I replied, looking out the window as I watched a couple of people walking through the park on their way over toward the stage. Seeing a homeless looking man sitting down at one of the trees near the stage, I said, "What's up with the random homeless guy?"

Everyone looked out the window as we parked.

Kane said, "That's Old Man Smiles, he's cool."

I asked, "Old Man Smiles? You know him?"

He nodded. "I'll introduce you. He's a nice guy."

Piling out of the car, Kane and I headed over to the tree that had the homeless man at it. Looking up at us, the man smiled warmly. "Good day to the both of you, what can I do for you?"

Kane smiled and said, "I wanted to introduce my buddy to you. Do you remember me from the restaurant back a while ago?"

The man rose up to his feet and squinted as he looked at Kane. "Oh, yes. How could I forget such a kind man? I was hungry and you put a twenty in my hand."

"You gave him twenty bucks?" I asked Kane, turning to him.

"Yeah," he replied. Kane looked at the guy and asked, "Did you feed your friends?"

"Oh yes... We ate like royalty under the bridge that

night, and for a moment of time, we had all forgotten we were without a home."

Kane nodded as he listened with intrigue.

"McCormick, Alderman!" Cole shouted from near the stage.

"It was nice seeing you again," Kane said, extending a hand to shake Old Man Smiles' hand.

"Nice meeting you," I said, shaking Old Man Smiles's hand.

On the way over to the stage, I looked back at the man again. He was strange, but he possessed a poetic way with words. I liked that.

"I need you two to help with the cases of water," Cole said as we approached him. "They're over there in that silver van." Cole pointed over to a van parked along side of the park that was a pretty good walking distance away.

Kane and I walked through the grass, headed for the vans. "That old guy was pretty cool, wasn't he?" Kane asked.

"Interesting, that's for sure. How'd he end up homeless?"

Kane shot a look over his shoulder back over to the

tree where the old man was. "I don't know—never asked. I don't see him a whole lot other than when I see him walking the streets and waving to cars."

"Mr. Taylor said he needed you over at the stage," a kid said, approaching me.

"Okay." I made my way over to Cole near the stage.

"Alderman," Cole said, dropping his clipboard to his side.

"Yeah, what is it?"

"We need to talk," he said, motioning me away from the growing crowd that was gathering in front of the stage.

"All right." Following him over to a quiet spot away from the crowd, I stood idly waiting for him to speak. A few minutes went by and I raised an eyebrow. "What?"

"So . . . we had a threat on the rally," he said. My ears began ringing as my heart raced out of control. Cole kept talking, but all I could think about was the kid and his threat. "What was the threat?"

"Someone said they planted a bomb in the park," Cole said. Noticing his eyes wander to my coat's side, I knew what he was looking at. "I have to ask. Do you know something we need to know?"

Shifting my step, I moved my arm to block the gun he was staring at in my pocket. "No."

"Just coincidence that you showed up with a gun today?" Cole knew something was up.

Stealing a glance of the crowd for a moment, I saw people. Residents, both young and old, and even a few children mixed in with the crowd. They were all there to support us.

Cole put his hand on my shoulder, "These people could be in danger, Alderman."

Nodding, I looked him dead in the eye. I let a long sigh come out from my lips. It felt like weight was shifting off my body as the words came out. "I got mixed up with some bad people, I'm afraid."

"What?" Cole scowled.

Shaking my head, I said, "He's just a kid. I don't think he'll do anything."

"Kid? How old?" Cole inquired.

"Like twenties? Maybe twenty-two or something," I said.

Cole looked over his shoulder at city hall and then

back at me. "Alderman. I'm calling this whole thing off."

"Cole," I said, grabbing his shoulder as he was about to leave.

He turned and shrugged my hand off my shoulder. His eyebrows furrowed. He said, "There isn't a choice in the matter, Rick!"

He darted over to the rest of the coordinators and I began to fume with anger—not at Cole, but at the kid. He was messing with my life now.

Seeing Susan pull up to the park, I headed over to the car and got in.

"What are you doing?" she asked.

Looking over at her, I shook my head. "They called it off."

"Why?"

She had no idea how loaded of a question that was.

"Bomb scare."

"That's ridiculous! It's probably just the mayor or her cronies messing with your rally! I'd still do it!" she demanded in all seriousness.

"It's not that simple, Susan." Reaching up, I pulled my seat belt down over my chest and latched it in.

"Yeah, it is." She looked out the windshield and must have spotted Cole. "I'm going to talk to Cole."

"No!" I shouted, grabbing her arm. "Just let it go, Susan. It's not going to change anything."

She shook her head and turned the car back on. "Just isn't right . . ."

"I know," I replied. When I looked out the window, I noticed there was a lot of work left to do with taking everything down. I said, "You can just go home. I'll stay and help clean up."

"I can help. There isn't anything pressing at home."

Having Susan involved with the cleanup and around Cole when he knew more truth than she did worried me. The risk of her finding everything out was greater now than ever. Looking at her, I said, "Just head home, dear, the guys got this."

She frowned slightly and said, "You don't want me here. I understand."

Touching her arm softly, I leaned in and said, "It's not that. I just feel it's best if it's just me and the guys. We are all pretty bummed, and I don't think having women here will let us vent that in a healthy way."

She pointed out Kristen and said, "Kane's girlfriend is helping."

"She's probably leaving pretty quickly."

"Okay," she replied, defeated. It tore me to pieces that she felt so unwanted, but her knowing the truth or the kid trying something with her in the park didn't sound good either. "Rick . . . can I at least go say 'hi' to Kristen? She's the one that suggested that lemon cake recipe we had the other day."

There wasn't a reason I could come up with to shoot it down. Nodding, I said, "Yeah, go ahead, dear, it was a wonderful cake."

Getting out of the car, we headed over to the stage. She veered off toward Kristen and I headed over to Cole. Interrupting his conversation with some of the workers, I said, "Hey man. Keep it quiet about my having the gun and knowing about the threat."

He furrowed his eyebrows. "What's going on, Alderman?" he demanded as the workers walked away.

Susan and Kristen came over to us with Kane. I widened my eyes at Cole to push the fact I didn't want him saying anything.

"That's not right that this all got shut down because of a threat, Cole," she said. "I was telling Rick I think it was probably the mayor's cronies behind it all."

Cole nodded slightly but didn't say anything. Instead, he turned and started conversing with the stage workers that he had previously been talking to.

Looking over at me, Kristen asked, "Did you like the cake?"

"Yeah, it was good cake." Looking over at Susan, I smiled.

"Well, I better get going," Susan said, pulling her keys out from her purse.

"Okay. It was nice seeing you again. Thanks for letting me know about the cake!" Kristen said.

"You're welcome. Thanks for the recipe!"

Going back over to the car, I shut the driver's side door after Susan got in. Leaning down to her open window, I said, "I'll be home in a few hours."

She smiled up at me. "I love you, Rick. You did a great thing here. It's too bad it didn't happen."

I leaned in and kissed her. "I love you too. Thank you."

Susan turned the key over and pulled forward out of

the spot she was parked in. Watching as she drove out of the park, I smiled. She was an amazing woman. I felt horrible about how much I had been hiding from her.

Cole came up to my side as I stood there and watched Susan pull forward out of the spot.

"You can't run from your lie for long," Cole said.

Turning to him, I said, "I'm trying to fix it."

"How much trouble are you in?" Cole asked.

"I respect you, Taylor. But I do not want to have this conversation. Okay?"

"Okay, but I want you to know I'll be praying for you." He turned and walked away, leaving me with my thoughts.

As we all were working together to dissemble the stage as the final step before being able to leave the park, my phone suddenly rang. "Here," I said to Kane's nephew, motioning for him to come over and grab the metal rod I was holding up.

He grabbed onto it as I pulled my phone out of my

pocket and walked away. It wasn't a number I recognized.

"Hello?"

"Mr. Aderman?" a woman's voice said on the other end.

"*Alder*man. Yes, it's me. Who is this?" My steps took me aimlessly across the grass.

"This is a nurse from Deaconess Hospital. Your wife was brought in about an hour ago—"

Sticking my neck out slightly, I shouted, "What? Are you kidding me right now? Is she okay?"

"She's doing great, considering what happened."

Cole tried to call out to me from over at the stage, but I wasn't paying attention. I walked further away.

"What happened?" I shouted into the phone as I squeezed the phone tightly in my hand.

"She ran a red light and was hit in the driver's side by a truck." My insides felt like they were in a furnace at the words.

Susan, I thought to myself. *Be okay.*

"She's been there for an hour already? Why didn't anyone call me?" I snapped at the nurse as I paced the grass in circles.

"Sir, she's okay. Mostly just scrapes and bruises. Can you please come down? She is asking for you, and she will need a ride home."

"Yeah. I'm already on my way," I said, hanging up the phone as I jogged over to Cole.

Cole walked up to me as I approached him. "What's going on?" he asked. "What's wrong?"

"Susan was in a wreck. I need to go see her."

"Take my car," Cole said, pulling out his keys and handing them to me.

"Y'all will be okay getting home?" I asked, looking over at the other guys.

"Yeah," Cole replied. "Between Kane's girlfriend and Micah's wife, we should have plenty of seats. Don't worry about us. Go see your wife."

"Thanks," I replied. Turning, I jogged over to the street where his car was parked.

"Rick!" Cole shouted as he walked through the grass to get in earshot of me.

Turning before getting into the car, I looked at him. "Give it to God," he said.

My lips pursed. Cole didn't get it. He had no idea how screwed up my life was in that moment.

Putting the car in reverse, I punched the gas and flew backward out of the parking spot. I braked hard, threw the SUV in drive and floored it, heading to the hospital to see Susan.

CHAPTER 12

The emergency room at Deaconess was packed. It
looked like an outbreak of a virus must have hit
Spokane, judging by the sea of people that were
stuffed into the waiting room. I made my way to the
line that led up to the front desk to get checked in. I
didn't see anyone else available that could let me
into the back. With every second that ticked by, my
patience grew thinner and thinner.

After a while, maybe ten or so minutes, I leaned
onto one foot and looked up the line toward the

desk.

"I just need to get into the back to see my wife."

"We all have needs, dude. You ain't special!" Some punk kid lashed out at me over his bulky shoulder.

"Excuse me?" I said, stepping out of line and walking up to him. He didn't acknowledge me. I tapped his shoulder.

He turned and looked at me. "What do you want?"

"I want you to repeat what you said to me." My fist was already clenched and ready to pummel the guy.

He glanced at my fist and then at me. "*I said*, 'we all have needs and you aren't special.'"

I cocked my arm and fist to swing, and someone from behind me grabbed my hand. Twisting around, about to clock the little punk, I saw it was Ron.

I shook my head and said, "Thought you were an old man and didn't have any strength left!"

"Thought you were an adult and had common sense!" He grabbed my shoulder and pulled me away from the line.

"What are you doing here?" I asked, looking at him.

"Don't you have some food to cook?"

"You better knock it off, Rick! You're not a kid

anymore!" He patted my side where the gun was. "You're packing heat that isn't registered to you and about to swing at a complete stranger in hospital, you moron! I gave you that gun to protect yourself, not to get caught with it in act of stupidity!"

My eyes went to the floor.

He put his hand on my shoulder.

"Look . . . I know that guy is screwing with you, Rick. And when I saw on the news what happened at your rally, I knew something wasn't right. Then, I called Cole up and found out about Susan. The nurse I spoke to on the phone at Deaconess said Susan is okay . . . you know that?"

"Yeah. How'd you find out about her?" I asked.

"I said I was family."

"Susan might be okay, but I'm not! I need to get back there to her, Ron!"

"You need to calm down. Take a breather," Ron said, patting my shoulder.

Ron led me up to the front of the line, past all the other people. Leaning over the counter, he asked, "Could you just open the doors? We are here to see someone."

"Sure," the woman from behind the desk replied. She reached over and hit a button on the wall that opened the doors for us.

"Thanks," Ron said. Turning to me, he said, "See? You just calm down . . . you can use your noggin."

Walking with Ron through the double doors that opened, we found our way to a nurses' station.

"Name, please," the lady at the station said without looking up at us.

Leaning on the counter, I said, "Susan. Susan Alderman."

She typed for a few moments and said, "Room 17." She stood up and pointed down the hall. "Just go down to the end of the hall and hang a left; it'll be the first room on your right." She sat back down.

"Thank you," I said.

She nodded, but she said nothing in response and went back to typing away on the keyboard.

Coming to Susan's door, Ron stopped me and said, "You go ahead in there. Just give me your jacket . . . so you're not walking around with my gun."

I took off the jacket and handed it to him. As I did, I said, "I'm sorry, Ron. I should have known that about the ER doors being opened easily like that. I should have just asked them to open them so I could come see her."

"It's okay. You're stressed and freaking out. We have a hard time thinking clearly during moments like this."

Nodding my head, I smiled at him and said, "Thanks for showing up like you did. You're a good man and a solid friend."

"Don't get all mushy on me." Ron laughed. He patted my shoulder and winked at me. "I just didn't want my gun to show up in a criminal case of a husband gone mad."

I laughed.

"Take care, Rick. Keep a level head between those shoulders."

Smiling as I pushed open the door to Susan's room, I saw her lying there, and reality came back to me in an instant.

My wife was in a car wreck.

She was hurt.

Frozen in place, I thought about all the things that could've happened. She could've been seriously hurt—she could've died. And I wasn't there to protect her, in fact, I was lying to her left and right, endangering her, and hurting her in my own way.

Rushing across the smooth hospital floor, I came to her bedside and grabbed her hand. Her eyes were shut.

"Susan!" I shook her hand. "Can you hear me?"

Her eyes blinked open. "Of course I can hear you. I was just sleeping. I don't even have an I.V. in my arm, Rick." She raised her arm up.

Looking her over, I saw that she wasn't even in a gown, just under a cover.

"I got cold," she said, seeing that I was looking at the blanket.

"Oh. Are you still cold? Do you need another blanket?"

"No, this is fine."

"I see. I hate to ask, but what happened, Susan? You're one of the best drivers I know. How did this happen?" I asked, sitting down on the edge of bed.

"I couldn't stop the car. I hit the brakes at the light, and the pedal just went straight to the floor of the car."

"You didn't notice on the way out of the parking lot?"

"I didn't have to use the brakes. There weren't any cars coming when I pulled out."

"What about on the way to the park? There had to be some indication?" I asked, confused.

"No, Rick, they were fine." Looking away from her, I looked at the floor as I thought about it. Then I remembered that Susan got out of the car for a few minutes. Shaking my head, I thought about Robert. He had to have been there, lurking off in the distance behind a tree or something. It sounded crazy even to me, but it had to be him. He must have been nearby and cut the brake lines. Susan sat up and put her hand on my arm.

"What are you thinking about, Rick?" she asked. "You look like you're debating something."

Looking her in the eyes, I couldn't tell her another lie. I cupped my face and couldn't hold back the tears. *This is going to break her heart, but I can't keep lying to her. This is getting out of control.*

"What's going on?" she demanded. "You're freaking me out!"

Shaking my head as I wiped my tears, I said, "It's bad. It's really bad, Susan."

"What do you mean? The doctors said I'll be fine." She leaned forward and looked out the door. Were they lying to me? That doctor rubbed me the wrong way. I'm an adult and I should be treated as one, it was the car's fault, not mine! You'd think I was crazy with the way they've acted toward me here."

I raised my hand, and she stopped. "No, Susan. It's not that."

"Then what, Rick?"

Turning to face her on the bed, I scooped up her hands from the blanket and held them in my lap. Fighting back tears, I looked her in the eyes.

"C'mon Rick, what is it?" she said, urging me on.

I took in a deep breath and let it escape my nose as I focused on her. *This is it. There aren't any other options left for me. My wife has been hurt, I have to tell her.*

My phone rang.

It was Cole.

Looking at her, I just couldn't tell her. This was a perfect opportunity to spill the truth about it all, and

I couldn't. Using the phone call as a needed excuse, I stood up and walked away from Susan's bed.

"Rick . . ." she said from the bed.

"Hold on," I said to her. "It's Cole."

"What's going on, Taylor?"

"We got back to the station and found a North Bend Casino poker chip sitting on your car. Does that mean anything to you?"

The kid. I have to stop this...

Any remaining doubts of him being the one behind this vanished in an instant. "Don't worry about it," I replied in a false state of calm. "I'll swing by the station here in a few and get your car back to you. I'll talk to you later."

I now knew where he was. He was at the casino. He was trying to draw me there, and it was going to work.

"I gotta go, honey," I said coming back over to her bed. Leaning in, I kissed her cheek. "I'll be back in a bit."

"Rick. What were you going to say? And you can't leave; they're releasing me within the next few minutes. I need you to take me home, they said. I don't have the car here, it's sitting over in a grocery store parking lot, plus they said I shouldn't drive on the medications they gave me anyway." She grabbed onto my hands. Her eyes were begging, pleading for me to just stay with her.

Anxiety began to rise in me. I had to get out there to the casino. I had to go find Robert, see him and get this fixed before he goes away into the shadows to torture me and the people I care about more.

"Honey. You just have to trust me." Thinking back to how upset she was about that one little poker night and not knowing anything, I feared the worst as the next few words came off my lips. "Call a cab, I'll see you later."

"Rick!" she shouted as I released myself from her hold and headed for the door. Her broken voice in that moment echoed in my head as I made my way to the door of her room.

I stopped at the doorway and looked back at my sweet and broken Susan as she had tears streaming down her cheeks, and her sadness about killed me. I could feel the sting of her disappointment, but I had to stop the kid.

Leaving the hospital, I swung by the fire station and dropped off Cole's car to him. I promptly got into my car and began driving north to the casino.

Getting to the poker tables, I scoped out the place. My heart was pounding as my eyes went from table to table, searching for the kid.

He was nowhere.

My jaw clenched.

"Where are you?" I said under my breath.

Walking farther into the poker area, I saw Joe. I saw that his table was on break, so I approached him and tapped his shoulder.

"Blaze," he said, reaching up with a hand to shake mine. We shook. "Haven't seen you around in a while," he said with softness in his tone.

"I know . . . some stuff came up. Hey, you remember that kid I played with the last time I was here?"

"Yep. He plays here all the time."

"I'm looking for him."

"He was here about an hour ago. You just missed

him," Joe said.

Standing up, I scanned the room again. He wasn't at any of the tables. I still couldn't see him anywhere.

"What's going on?" Joe asked.

Patting his shoulder, I said, "Too complicated to discuss. Take care. And thanks, Joe." Walking past Joe, I headed out the back exit of the casino and stood near the curb.

"Where are you?" I said, dropping down to sit on the curb.

Click.

The sound of a gun from behind me froze me in place. Feeling its presence right behind me, I stood up and raised my hands in the air. I began to turn, but the gun's tip pushed into my back.

"Don't move," someone said, stepping closer and jabbing the gun into my back. "And put your hands down, this isn't a movie."

It was Robert.

"What do you want? Whatever you want, I'll give it to you. Just stop torturing me and ruining my life!"

He laughed. "I guess you're one of those people that just needs a little motivation to get moving in the right direction, eh?"

I remained silent. *How did I let it come to this?*

He grabbed my shoulder and shoved the gun into my back again. "We're going on a little trip to see Lincoln. Remember him? He's not going to come across quite as nice this time, though. He's a little upset with you."

"Why? Because you lied to me about the stupid buy-in? I thought you took care of it."

The kid laughed as he began leading me down the sidewalk, away from the lights and out into the parking lot. My heart began pounding in my chest as we went deeper into the darkness.

"He was trying to keep this simple," the kid said.

"What? This was a con?" Thinking back to the run-in with the kid at the diner, it was rather soon after the casino trip. Then the whole buy-in fiasco flashed through my mind. It all started to click. They set me up, and for what? I was a good guy, an average Joe just trying to make a living and raise a family. I didn't have anything.

"Man, you are slow, old man," the kid replied, laughing as we came to an RV. He pulled the gun from my back and used the butt of it to knock on the door. "Don't try nothing in here. If you want to see Susan again—alive."

My jaw clenched at his threat. I'd never contemplated murdering somebody for real before, but if I got close, it was right then in that moment. The door opened. It was Bear, the guy from the poker night in the Valley. He looked like his usual unfriendly self.

We stepped up into the RV. The screen door was broken and it hung crooked on the frame. We went inside and past Bear on the way to a room in the back. Entering the room, the kid shut the door behind me and locked it. My heart continued to beat so hard that I could feel it thumping in my ears. The room was large and cozy for being in an RV, but it didn't do anything for my nerves. I looked over toward a chair in the back corner, and there sat Lincoln.

Standing up, he shook his head. "You know, Rick," he said as he stepped toward us and lowered an eyebrow as he glared. "I thought you were smart." He raised a hand out to his side and let the palm rest upwards as he continued to talk. "You know, a man of honor, being a firefighter and all."

"Don't disrespect me! You're not one to talk about honor!" I lashed out at him.

He came closer and turned away from me, only to return with the back of his hand across my face.

"You fool!" he shouted, taking a step back. "Don't you understand yet? Or maybe we need to go for your daughter . . . Bethany, is it? Maybe you haven't quite grasped how serious I am."

I lunged toward Lincoln as I let out a deep yell. "I'll kill you!" I shouted as the kid grabbed onto my shoulder and pulled me back.

Lincoln laughed. "I'd kill you right now if I could, you stupid, old man . . . but I'd rather watch you suffer." He pointed over to the wall and said, "Watch."

A video came up of a restaurant. Beth was sitting alone eating a meal, and my heart started pounding. Then, the kid came up to the table and sat down. They were conversing like they knew each other.

"What is this? You have been videotaping my daughter? Who are you, the mob?" I asked, watching the screen.

Lincoln looked over at me. "Robby here likes your daughter."

"Well, she's happily married," I retorted.

"Yeah. But Robby is helping her with tutoring for . . . what's your granddaughter's name?"

I didn't respond.

Robert said, "Natalie."

I jerked again, but the kid dug his fingers deeper into my shoulder. It hurt. Oh man, did it hurt. His boney little fingers were like daggers in my skin. I wondered why he didn't just shoot me. I would have almost preferred it by the kind of day I was having.

"What do you want from me?" I demanded.

"Just what you agreed to pay."

"I gave you the two grand already!" I shouted back at him.

"You sure are stupid, aren't you?" Lincoln asked.

"Look. We know you have eighty grand in the bank. We just want a very small portion of that."

I laughed.

Lincoln asked, "What's so funny?"

I shook my head and replied, "Your facts are *old*. I

don't have that kind of money anymore."

Lincoln stepped up to me. "You're lying."

"I'll show you my bank account."

He looked over at the kid. The kid shrugged and said, "The information *was* from four years ago."

"Shut up," Lincoln said as he turned and went around the chair. He leaned on the back and looked intensely at me. "You've been coming to the tables a long time, always playing and spending."

"Yeah, I was draining the account."

"I hope you're wrong," Lincoln said softly.

"Why?" I asked.

He came back over to the wall and said, "If you're telling the truth, I will kill your daughter."

"Wait!" I shouted.

"What?" he turned to me.

"I have about fourteen thousand dollars. You add that to the two thousand, and that's sixteen thousand."

"That a boy," Lincoln said, grinning as he walked over to me. He grabbed onto my face with a hand and squeezed my cheeks between his fingers. "That wasn't so difficult to find money, Mr. Fireman, now was it? Unfortunately, the price just went up. It's thirty thousand now for making me mad."

"Okay. I'll find the money. I'm going to need to go get it, though." I looked over at the video on the wall that was the recording of my daughter, Beth. I shook my head. Getting out of the RV alive and keeping my family alive was all that mattered in that moment. I would sell everything if I had to, even the clothes on my back, to get these guys away from us. Lincoln looked over at the kid.

"I think he's well motivated." The kid laughed.

"Good." Lincoln looked at me. "That address that Robby gave you—drop it off there. Nine o'clock tonight. Don't make the same mistake twice, or it will be more than a couple of snipped brake lines for precious Bethany." Lincoln walked back to his chair, sat down, and waved his hand, signaling for us to leave.

The kid grabbed me and led me out of the room, a gun still firmly pressed into my back. On the way out of the RV, the kid said, "Don't try anything with the cops. I've seen Lincoln kill."

When we reached the exit where Bear was standing,

he grabbed me and tossed me out the door. I landed hard onto the pavement. Before I had time to even look back, the door slammed shut.

CHAPTER 13

My trembling hands gripped the steering wheel when I got back into my car. Disturbed didn't begin to describe how I felt inside. I was freaking out. I hurried down the freeway back toward Spokane. My pulse was racing and my heart was pounding. In all my years on this earth, I had never been in a worse situation. Not even the worst fires shook me up like this. No, this was my family, my life. I was almost back to Spokane, and I couldn't take it anymore. I pulled along the side of the highway.

My wheels rode along the sleeper until I pulled entirely off the road and parked. Bowing my head, I prayed.

"Dear God," I said, looking up at the ceiling of my car. I dropped my head against the steering wheel and a few tears came rolling down my cheeks. "I can't do this. I don't know what to do anymore. And I know . . ." The tears came on more as I lifted my eyes. My hands and heart trembled in fear as flashes of my wife's scrapes and bruises pressed against my mind. "I know I haven't been to church in a while and I'm sorry." I looked out the window. A semi-truck zoomed by, shaking the car. I thought of my daughter, Beth, and the grandkids. "Please protect my family. It is only you that knows how this will end. Please, Lord. Amen."

I put the car into drive and checked my side mirror before pulling back out onto the freeway. I wiped the tears from my eyes. I was unable to stop checking the rearview mirror. I was paranoid. I sped all the way down the interstate back to Spokane. The fear that was crippling me before I prayed began to fade, and a peace washed over me. I was still worried, but I felt that God was with me.

Seeing my turn off up ahead, I debated on going home to my wife. *She'll want answers*, I thought to myself. I wasn't ready to give her any, not yet. She'd go straight to the police.

Passing the exit home, I continued onward.

Ron. I'll see go see Ron.

Taking the next exit, I drove through town to Heidi's diner. It was around eight o'clock. Closing time soon. With only moments to spare, I pulled into the parking lot.

Ron was sitting outside in the back. His hands were folded together, and he was seated on an upside-down milk crate. Pulling right up in front of him, I parked and got out. His head lifted and our eyes met.

"I suspect you didn't come for a bite to eat?" he asked, standing up as I approached.

"This whole problem is a lot worse than I thought. They know everything, man. Robert –that punk kid, has been hanging out with Beth! Tutoring Natalie!" I ran my fingers through my hair and shook my head.

More tears fell.

"Calm down, Rick," Ron said. "Tell me what happened."

"I met with the kid at the casino. He put a gun in my back and led me to Lincoln, the head honcho, in some RV that was out in the parking lot of the casino." Thinking about the video of Beth, I lost it and kicked a nearby garbage can as hard as I could.

Ron put a hand on my shoulder and said, "It's okay. It's okay, man."

Shaking my head, I said, "It's not okay! They think I have all this money that I don't have anymore. I spent it all, man." Tears fell again. "I don't know what to do!"

"What do they want?"

"They want what I owe them, plus more because I've made them mad! They're conning me. I'm freaking out, man. They hurt Susan!" My lips pursed. "And they're going after Beth next if I don't pay! I don't even have half of what they want."

Ron remained calm, which helped my nerves. In a smooth and controlled voice, asked, "How much?"

"Thirty thousand," I said.

He squinted as he pondered something, and then he reached into his pocket. Fishing out the keys to his GTO, he handed them to me and said, "That car is worth more than that."

"I can't take that," I said, pushing the keys back to him.

"Rick," he said. He pushed the keys back to me. "Take the car."

"Why would you do that for me?" I asked, shaking my head.

"Rick, you have been like a son to me. I'm nearing the end of my life, and every day I wake up is a blessing. I'm always on the lookout for how I can help. You know that. Let me do this for you. It's the only way this is going to stop."

Looking at the keys in my hand, I shook my head again. "I don't deserve this."

"It's a gift, Rick," he said. "Don't you get that? It's not about earning it." He covered his mouth and coughed. "Take it!"

Thinking about my baby girl being in danger and thinking of my wife getting hurt earlier that day all came to a point. My only chance of freedom from this disaster was Ron's car.

"Okay." Looking at him, I said, "Thank you. You think this will work?"

"If they know anything at all about cars, it will."

"How do I drop a car off? By myself?" I asked. "And what will you do without a car?"

"I have other cars. And just take a taxi back here to pick up your car." Ron put his hand on my shoulder and said, "Remember . . ." He pointed to his head. "You gotta be calm to think clearly. And by the way, before you ask, the title is in the glove box. I'll walk with you and sign the title before you leave." He smiled at me. "Stay calm."

"I don't know how to ever thank you, Ron."

"Stop this madness, and fix your relationship with God and your wife." Ron turned and looked up at the big sign over the diner that said his wife's name—Heidi. "I miss her every day, and if I could go back, I'd do many things differently. The thing about *time* is that once it's gone, it's gone forever, and we never know how much we have left. Oftentimes, it's less than we think."

"I promise I'll make it all right." Looking at my

watch, I said, "I'm going home to see Susan and then to go finish this."

I drove home using city streets instead of the freeway. It gave me a little more time to take it slow and start thinking clearly. My wife was going to be home and fuming.

I'm going to tell her the whole truth.

No matter how badly it hurt, I was going to tell her. Pulling up to the house, I saw an unknown maroon sedan sitting in the driveway. My heart started pounding as I feared the worst. *It's not nine, yet. Did they decide not to wait? Please let her be okay!*

Bolting inside, I came into the living room. To my relief, my pastor and one of the deacons were sitting on the couch. Susan was in the recliner, folded over into her hands with tears running down her face. All eyes shifted over to me.

"Rick," pastor Conner said as I tried to turn and leave.

I turned back around to find him already off the couch and approaching me with a distorted and concerned look on his face. "Where are you going?" he asked.

"That's a long story," I said, looking past him at Susan as she wiped her face with a tissue that she'd fetched from a box on the coffee table. My heart ached to see her pain drawn out across her face in the form of red, swollen eyes and tears. "Glad to see you made it out of the hospital," I added, hoping to shift the direction.

"Thanks. But we aren't here to talk about me. We're here for you," the pastor said.

"You don't understand," I replied, trying to maintain my composure.

"Help me understand." The pastor turned to face Susan on the recliner. "Help your wife understand what is going on."

"With all due respect, I don't feel like *right now* is a good time for this," I replied.

"That's not fair to Susan," Pastor Conner said softly, dipping his chin.

"You have no right!" I snapped at him.

"You're a Biblical Christian, Rick. Don't forget that. You know I have every right to shepherd the flock. It's my duty as the pastor of our congregation. I'm here at your house because your wife called me here.

I'm here to help."

"Okay." I took a deep breath in and let it out. Glancing at my watch, I saw that it was twenty minutes until nine. "But right now, I have to go."

Pastor Conner put his hand on my shoulder. "Rick. Please come sit down with us and talk."

My jaw clenched and I said through my teeth, "I can't."

"Why?" Susan asked, standing up from the recliner. She came across the floor and up to me. "Tell me why, Rick." Tears streamed down her cheeks as she pleaded for an explanation.

"Come with me, and I'll explain on the way," I offered, trying to fix this. I reached for her hand, but she pulled it away.

"I'm not going anywhere with you," she replied. "Are you in some sort of trouble? Let's call the police. They'll help you."

Turning, I went for the door. I couldn't tell her. The police would ruin everything. As I grabbed the doorknob, Susan grabbed my arm. I stopped and looked at her for a moment. "Susan . . ." I said, my voice breaking. In all our years, I swore I would never hurt her. *Lord, please let her forgive me.*

"Let him go do what it is that he thinks he needs to do," the pastor said. Susan let go of my arm.

Opening the door, I gently pulled my arm from her and ran out to the GTO.

Arriving to the address, I was surprised to see it was a house. It looked vacant. A board was missing from one of the windows in the front and the lights were all off, except the front porch light. That was illuminated and lit up the top step of the cement stairs.

I got out of the GTO and walked up the empty driveway as I phoned for a cab to head in my direction. Turning off the driveway and down the path, I walked up to the front door. It was pitch dark inside the house, but I gave it a few good knocks to see if anyone was around and then took a step back. No surprise, nobody answered.

Reaching into the mailbox that hung next to the door, I brought the mail into the light. It was post marked for over two years ago. I sighed and replaced the mail back in the box. Walking back down the steps, I looked down the street both ways on my way back to the car.

Then a black car rounded the corner just up the block. It pulled up and stopped in the middle of the street, right outside the house. The window rolled down back and the kid stuck his head out. "Bring the money?" he asked.

"I have something better," I said, pointing to the GTO.

"That's a mistake," the kid said, rolling up the window.

I sprinted up to the car and knocked on the window, shouting, "Wait!"

The window went back down.

"Listen," I said. I pointed over to Ron's car that I'd driven to the house. "That's a 1964 Pontiac GTO—"

"That doesn't mean anything to me," the kid retorted.

"It's worth well over the $30,000 you want from me." He looked over at the car for a moment, and then said, "Hold on." The window went back up. My heart pounded for what felt like hours as I waited. I could see him faintly through the tinted window as he talked on the phone.

The window didn't come back down. Instead, the kid opened the door and said, "You got lucky." He began walking over to the car and ran a finger along the side of it as he inspected the car.

"We even now?" I asked.

The kid stopped near the front of the car and paused. He turned around to me and said, "Keys? Clean title?"

I lobbed the keys up in the air toward him and he caught them. "Title is in the glove box."

He nodded. "As long as the car is fine, we're good."

Relief came over me as I thought of my wife and daughter. They were finally safe.

Cops suddenly came flying around the corner, and as they did, the sirens and lights came on. The kid glared over at me. "You called the cops! You idiot! Your family is as good as dead now!" he shouted, sprinting back to the car he had come in.

The black car took off down the street and whipped around the corner, the cops chasing after it. One of the patrol cars stopped along the curb just outside the house and got out.

"No! Wait! I didn't call them!" I yelled frantically, watching as the car vanished out of sight. "Who called the cops?" I asked as the cop got out and walked up to me.

"Can I get your name, Sir?" he asked, clicking the pen in his hand to start writing.

"Rick Alderman. Who called you?" I asked, seeing the cab pull up to the curb.

"Don't get hostile with me, sir," he replied. "We're the good guys. I just responded to a call."

"Let me go tell the cab driver to leave," I said. Leaving the officer, I went over to the cab and let him know I wasn't going to need a ride and that he could leave.

I shook my head as I walked back up to the officer and looked down the road. It must have been my paranoia kicking in again like back at the fire station, because I spotted a car pulling away. I strained my vision to get a good look at the car and noticed that it looked similar to Cole's vehicle. "Did Cole Taylor call it in?" I asked.

"I can't discuss that with you. So tell me what happened."

"What?"

"Tell me what happened?"

"Starting from when?" I asked, shrugging.

The cop adjusted his footing as an eyebrow shifted down. "From the beginning, Mr. Alderman."

"First off, I need to know my wife and daughter are going to be safe. They need protection from the people who are after me."

"We can send a patrol car by," he replied.

"No. That's not going to do it. You don't understand."

The officer's eyebrows furrowed and he crossed his arms. "What do you mean?"

"Promise me they'll be safe!" I demanded.

"I'll do whatever I can to protect them."

"Okay," I replied, satisfied. I had to trust him. I took a deep breath and started from the night at the casino. I told him everything.

CHAPTER 14

Sneaking my way into the house late that night, I

crashed on the couch for fear of waking Susan. I was going to tell her, but the last thing I wanted to do was get into a long conversation with her when I had to be up the next morning for work.

When my eyes blinked open the next day to my alarm clock on my phone, I leaped up and checked out the window to make sure the unmarked cop car was still sitting outside. It was. Turning around, I was surprised by the absent smell of coffee coming from the kitchen. Sitting up, I stretched. *She must have had a rough night again*, I thought to myself as I got up.

Tiptoeing up the stairs to our bedroom, I found my way to the door and peeked in. I noticed the bed was made.

"That's strange," I said, turning around and making my way back downstairs to the kitchen. Running the faucet in the sink, I glanced out the window that overlooked the backyard.

Seeing movement in the guest house, my heart began pounding. Was that Robert? No. It couldn't be. The cop last night said they picked him up a few blocks away. Another thug of Lincoln's? Did they sneak past the cop?

With the coffee pot still in my hand, I went out onto the back porch and down the steps into the yard.

Approaching the guest house with caution, I kept my arm cocked back, ready to smash the glass coffee pot over anyone's head I could find.

I turned the doorknob and pushed open the door to the guest house that led into the kitchen.

"Get out of here!" I shouted without going inside.

"Oh hush!" Susan said from the living room of the guest house, just beyond kitchen.

"Susan? What are you doing out here?" I asked, relaxing my arm as I walked inside.

"I slept out here last night."

Relaxing more, I set the coffee pot down on the kitchen table. "You're not staying out here."

She came in from the living room and said, "I most certainly am."

"You're not making sense." I crossed my arms. "What is this about, Susan? Because of last night?"

She turned her head and looked out to the backyard.

"You used to be a man I admired . . . and now . . . I don't know where you go or with whom, or what you're doing . . ." She paused.

I knew she was right. *I need to tell her everything.*

She looked over at me with tear-filled emerald eyes and continued. "You're a stranger."

I grabbed her hand as I felt my heart crumble at seeing her sadness. "Susan, you know me! I'm still that guy you love! I'll tell you everything! I won't hold anything back!"

She sniffled. "I saw the bank account."

I let go of her hand, letting it fall back to her side.

"I can explain."

She shook her head. "You spent our savings! Seventy thousand dollars, Rick."

"I know. That wasn't right. But here's what happened—"

"Stop!" she shouted. "We used to talk about twenty dollar purchases when we were younger. What was even going through your mind?"

"Hey, now!" I snapped back at her. "Look at all this *stuff* that fills the guest house. We didn't talk about that!"

She laughed under her breath. "What . . . *maybe* six grand worth of stuff in here. I lost my MOTHER! What is your excuse?! Because as far as I'm concerned, there is nothing you can say to excuse yourself. You spent seventy thousand dollars, Rick!"

Cringing at her tone with me, my lips pressed tightly together. I was trying to tell her, but she wouldn't let me explain.

She said, "You're not the man I married, this is not what I signed up for. I want you out! I don't want to see you! If I thought I could kick you out of here I would, but you're a stubborn man, so I'll just live out here! I will not share the same roof as you!" Her words cut through me. They cut deep. Susan's lip tightened and she stormed out of the guest house. She stuck her head back in through the doorway for one more jab, and said, "I don't know who you are anymore, Rick Alderman."

I went over to the doorway of the guest house and watched as she left through the side gate in the fence. She was burning with anger.

Rubbing my chin with the top of my palm, I went back toward the house. My body ached and I felt like I'd suddenly aged fifty years. The one person I cared about the most in the world felt like she didn't even know me, but the thing was—I didn't know myself either.

Defeated, I dragged myself into the house and up the stairs to the bedroom. I laid out my clothing on the bed for work and got in the shower. The grime and sweat washed away from my body and made their way down the drain, but the regret and guilt seemed to stick, and soap wasn't going to do the job.

The fire station's bright and usually colorful red
paint outside seemed a little dimmer that morning
as I arrived for work. And while my body was
arriving for work, my mind lingered elsewhere. It
was searching for how to make everything right with
Susan, searching for solutions to the problems I'd
caused. Distracted in my thoughts, I didn't even
notice Cole in the hallway when I arrived at the top
of the stairs in the fire house.

"Alderman," Cole said, startling me out of my
thoughts.

I glanced up at him and asked, "What is it, Taylor?"

"You saw me last night. Didn't you?"

Taking a deep breath as I unlatched my mind from
my thoughts, I recalled seeing him pull away from
the curb. "Yep," I replied, and then cleared my
throat. "You have some nerve sticking your nose in
my business, Taylor!" I blurted out.

"You should be thanking me, not yelling at me!"
Cole retorted, crossing his arms as he positioned his

feet shoulder length apart from one another.

"I was finally going to be done with these . . . these vile men, and you went and screwed everything up!" I snapped at him as I stepped closer. I got right up in his face. "You jeopardized not only my life, but those who I care about most. So I guess if you want a 'thank you' for that, here it is, buddy: Thank you for ruining everything. You may have thought you were helping, Cole, but it wasn't helpful!"

Cole's face went red from the top of his forehead down his neck. He was speechless.

I left the hallway and went into the kitchen to get a cup of coffee. Taking my cup, I headed back through the hallway over to the multi-purpose room. By that time, Cole was gone from the hallway. I took a seat on the couch next to Ted. He was pretty entranced with the television. There was some political coverage on the president. I sat there for a bit, not really paying attention to the TV. Just thinking, praying and hoping that I could find the right way to tell Susan and figure out a way to make this work.

"He's a Muslim," Ted said suddenly.

"Oh, yeah," I said, barely paying attention to him.

"Rick," Cole said from the doorway.

"What?" I asked, finding it strange that he used my first name.

He turned and nodded down the hall as he left.

Sighing, I said, "Guess I better follow?" Getting up a little too quickly, something tweaked in my back again. "Ugh," I said, followed by a grunt.

"Old man," Ted laughed from beside me on the couch.

I smiled. "You owe be twenty bucks, by the way. Mariners won."

He smiled. "That was a bad game. I don't have cash on me right now. I'll bring it in."

"A win's a win, right?" I replied.

"True that," he replied, returning his eyes to the TV.

Going out into the hallway, I saw Cole walking toward the sliding glass door in the dining hall. "Oh, great. A lecture."

Cole stopped and waited for me. Coming up to him, I raised my eyebrows.

"What is this? Some lecture? I don't need it, Cole. I'm over fifty years old."

His eyes narrowed on me. "You're right. You are

fifty-three years old, man." He took a deep breath. "Tell me about these shady dudes you were dealing with. I can put in a good word over at the police station with the guys over there.

"Don't worry about it. Just stay out of my way."

He shook his head.

"You don't understand, Taylor."

He pushed his right index finger into my chest. "No. You don't understand!" He adjusted his footing as he lowered his voice. "The mayor is moving forward with the cuts. There's going to be loss across the board. Not just here, but over at the police department too. If you're in trouble, let's get a couple of extra guys in blue to look into it while they still have the resources to do so."

My anger fell away immediately and was replaced by sadness. "The leader's name was Lincoln. Jet black hair, parted to one side. Small mustache and a cigar always hanging from his lips. The kid, Robert, who helped him, was picked up last night." My thoughts fell away from my drama as I turned and saw Brian in the kitchen. I lowered my voice. "Who's getting axed?"

He jotted down my description of Lincoln on a piece of paper and shoved it in his pocket. Quietly, he leaned in and replied, "Gomer, he's newest. Then . . . well, that's what I needed to talk to you about."

"What does that mean? Don't tell me my pension—"

Cole opened the sliding door and bowed his head for me to go first. Walking through the door, I kept looking back at Cole.

"What, Cole? I'm not losing my pension . . . am I?"

"Of course not," Cole said, taking a seat in one of the chairs out on the patio.

I joined him at the table and pulled my chair up close. "What's going on, Cole?"

"We were able to get the pensions left alone," he said.

I felt relieved.

"But what we need to talk about is early retirement," Cole said, bringing his hands together on the table. "Micah will be taking early retirement next year, and you can take it now, if you want."

Leaning back in my chair, I asked, "What's the alternative?"

"We cut more from the crew," Cole said softly. "You

were already going to be retiring in a couple of years; this just gives you a jump start."

I stared at him with a blank face. Retirement from working was something I'd looked forward to for many years; it was going to be more time with Susan. But with our strained relationship, I worried what retirement would look like now if things were to stay the same.

"I'll give you a few days to talk to Susan about it."

I laughed as I shook my head and glanced over the railing of the balcony that sat beside our table. "She left."

"She moved out?"

"Kind of." I looked over at Cole. "She moved into the guest house."

"I don't really know all that happened, Alderman, but I do know a few things. You love God, you love your wife, and you love this job. This job is soon ending. I'd suggest figuring things out between the other two loves in your life."

"I know," I replied. "I just don't know how to fix things."

"God is always the answer."

My phone rang. It wasn't a number I recognized. Standing up, I said, "I'll talk to you later, Taylor." Stepping away from the table, I answered it.

"This is Pastor Conner."

"Oh." Part of me wanted to hang up right then, but I respected the man too much to not hear him out.

"Before you hang up, I want to ask you something."

"Make it good. I'm at work."

"Okay. How would you feel about coming in for some counseling? For you and Susan?"

"Susan put you up to this? I bet she did. She thinks she can just steamroll—"

"No," he said, interrupting me.

"What? You just dreamed this up on your own?" I asked, walking down to the end of the balcony.

"No. I saw you two at the house the other day."

I laughed. "You don't even understand what was going on."

"I don't need to. Listen: come meet with me for a half hour sometime this week and let's talk."

"I don't know what Susan's schedule is."

"Not her this first time. Just you."

"I don't like your aggressiveness, Pastor Conner. I

find it uncomfortable and a bit brash."

He was silent for a moment. "Rick. I've known you for a long time, and I know what you respond to. You might not like it, but this type of communication is what works. Just meet with me this Thursday, if that works for you. At 2pm."

He was right. There wasn't much more that I didn't like in this world than a person who didn't have the nerve to speak directly. "I have to work. Let's do Saturday. 2pm."

"That's fine. See you then. At my office, in the church."

"See you then."

Hanging up the phone, I stared out at the city of Spokane as I rested my arms on the railing. This city wasn't going to be under my watchful eye for much longer, and if I wanted to enjoy these final years of my life, I knew a good relationship with my wife and my God were crucial. The idea of her spending my last years in the guest house made me feel sad more than anything else. A separated life wasn't what I desired for us.

Up in Smoke

CHAPTER 15

Saturday soon arrived. Susan and I hadn't spoken
more than a few words to each other all week. She
kept to herself out in the guest house. I hadn't even
told her about the news of the early retirement. I
figured she wouldn't care or she'd show little
interest in the information. After all, she was
becoming quite accustomed to the new
arrangement. The other night, I spotted a few of her
friends over in the kitchen. They sat around the

table playing bridge and chatting it up. She appeared happy, and it pained me. It also hurt how easy it was for her to not be in our house, in our own home. I, on the other hand, refused to believe this was the new way of living.

One of my eyes stayed partially shut as I ran the water in the sink to make a pot of coffee that early Saturday morning. Staring out the window as I let the water fill the pot, I saw the lights off in the guest house. I didn't like her being out there, but if she wasn't going to be living with me, it was the best place for her. I still worried about her safety, though. And that of my daughter. Sure, the kid was locked up, but that didn't mean anything. Lincoln was still out, and he still had plenty of muscle in his pocket.

The phone on the wall rang. Stopping what I was doing, I set the pot down and went to answer it. It was my daughter, Beth.

"Hey, Beth."

"Hi, Dad." Her words sounded strained and worried.

"What's going on?" I asked, leaning against the wall in the kitchen next to the phone.

"It's Philip. He's sick."

"Oh? What's wrong?"

"He has a fever that won't come down. I haven't ever seen anything like it. Is Mom there?"

We hadn't told Beth about anything. She was in the dark. My eyes lifted up toward the French doors that led out the back and to the guest house. "Let me go find her," I said.

Letting the phone dangle there against the wall, I headed out the double doors and out to the guest house. She didn't answer the door. I opened the door and called out for Susan as I went through the kitchen and into the living room.

She wasn't there.

Checking the two bedrooms, she wasn't there either. I began to worry. Jogging out of the house, I went through the gate and to the driveway. Her car was parked.

I went up the front steps of the house and back inside to the phone. "I don't know where she is, Beth."

"What do you mean you don't know where she is? Did you check the laundry room?" Beth asked.

I sighed. "She isn't here."

"How come you didn't just tell me that from the beginning, Dad?"

"I didn't know."

"How did you not know that Mom wasn't home?"

A child's scream came through the phone. It was opportunity to escape the conversation. "You sound busy. I'll have her call you when I see her." Hanging up the phone, I ran a hand through my hair as worry began to take the steering wheel of my mind once again. Was it Lincoln? Did she get kidnapped? Heading back to the front door, I peered down both directions of the street.

Then I heard a noise from inside the house and I heard the French doors from the kitchen shut.

I ran through the house and back to the kitchen. I was relieved to see it was Susan.

"Where were you?" I asked.

"Why?"

"Beth called."

Susan sighed. "We need to tell her."

I put a hand up as I came over to Susan. "We can wait. We don't need to tell her right now."

"For what? This is our life now until I get into a new

place."

"A new place?" I asked, surprised. "What's wrong with the guest house?"

"I don't need your watchful eyes on me. I see you peeking out at me all the time. Marge thought you were being super creepy the other night when we were playing bridge."

"Marge said that?" Shaking my head and hurt by the comment, I said, "She knows me. Why would I be creepy to her?"

"I don't know, Rick. I'm moving. I already have a place lined up. It's available in the beginning of November."

"Don't do that," I pleaded.

"You can't stop me. I'm not yours to control," she retorted. She grabbed for the door handle to leave, but paused. Looking back at me, she said, "I want that washer and dryer, by the way. I'm getting tired of waiting until you're at work."

"Why are you being so cruel?" I asked.

She let go of the handle and walked over to me.

"Don't you think it was cruel what you did, Rick? You left me in the dark. Not for a day or a week, but years. You lied to my face daily. You stole from us. You won't even tell me the full story! You're a liar and a thief, and I don't know how you live with yourself, but I'm glad I don't have to anymore!"

I could see through her cruelty and saw the pain behind her eyes. She was trying to keep a strong outward appearance, but I knew her too well. "I'm sorry for what happened, Susan," I said in a soft tone as I lightly grabbed onto her arm.

She brushed my hand away and turned to leave.

"Where did you go?"

"When?"

"When I was looking for you . . . when Beth was on the phone a few minutes ago."

"Went for a walk," she said with a soft and hopeless kind of tone. She turned and headed back to the door and left. Watching her as she shut the door behind her and walked across the deck, my heart hurt for what I'd done to her.

Pulling my car into a spot in the church's parking

lot, a flood of memories came rushing into my mind. This church housed memories that spanned decades. Beth's baby dedication, me leading the men's Sunday school class, and our family growing up. Susan and I even led the youth group for a few years. We were so active and a part of the church family back in our younger years. Then it all changed. It was a slow fade, starting when we shipped Beth off to college. We stopped volunteering as much, and then we started to cut our church attendance to only Sunday mornings, eventually stopping altogether.

Getting out of my car, I headed for the front doors of the church. The parking lot was rather empty that day, and a chilly breeze was blowing in from the south. I pushed my hands into my jeans as I hurried my steps across the pavement.

I felt nervous that day. Not because I had a beef with God, but because I knew how out of control my life had gotten without Him steering it. God was a big part of my life at one point, and for many years, and now, He had a special little box in the recesses of my mind. It had only been a couple of months since I'd attended church, but I hadn't let God steer my life in over a decade.

Going inside, my nerves settled as I made my way to pastor Conner's office. Church always had a calming effect on my soul. It was the one place in the world that made sense to me.

Pastor Conner's door was open as I approached it. I stuck my head in. He motioned me in and stood up, saying, "Come in, come in."

Stepping into the room, I reached across his desk and shook his hand. The top of his desk was littered with notes, Bibles, a calendar and even a few sticky notes with scribbles on them that I couldn't make out. "You look busy," I said. Glancing over my shoulder back toward the door, I said, "I can come back."

"No, no, Rick. This is what I like to call *organized chaos*." He laughed as he moved a few of the Bibles and notes to the side. "How are you?" he asked, taking a seat.

I laughed. "Yeah, it's a mess. I'm fine." I sat down.

"I mean it. How are you, Rick? This isn't a greeting where you just say 'fine' and keep walking. I'm genuinely interested in how you're doing."

"Well . . ."I replied as I processed the question. Scrambling through my thoughts, I couldn't really give an answer, so I shrugged.

"Let's try this." The pastor put his hands on his table and said, "What hurts?"

I furrowed my eyebrows.

"You gotta open up, Rick."

"Okay . . . my wife left," I replied. My nose scrunched up as I sniffed. "She just up and left, and there's nothing I can do about it."

The pastor pulled one of the Bibles from the stack he had and set it on the desk. He opened it up and spent a couple of minutes searching, thumbing through the pages. Then he stopped, cleared his throat, and asked, "May I read something to you?"

I nodded. "Go ahead. But I don't think it'll do much."

"You still believe in the Bible and God, don't you?" he asked.

"Yes," I replied, annoyed by his accusation. "But I've been through the Bible multiple times." I laughed. "You know that."

"Well, the power is in the Word, Rick." His eyes

went back down to the pages and he began to read. "In this same way, husbands ought to love their wives as their own bodies. He who loves his wife loves himself. Ephesians 5:28"

I tightened my lips as I furrowed my eyebrows at the pastor. "This isn't the problem, here."

He set the Bible down on the desk. "Go on."

"I lied to her. Betrayed her. And it went on for years."

"Mind me asking what you did?"

I hesitated for a second, but I knew I needed to confide in someone. So I spilled the beans. "I drained our savings account from eighty grand down to ten. Then I hid it from her. I was gambling it away."

"Why'd you feel like you could do it?" Pastor Conner asked, bringing his hands together. His expression was soft, and he seemed genuinely interested and not just trying to pry.

"I spent my whole life serving. I have served Spokane as a firefighter, my family as a dad and husband, and God as a volunteer in the church. I just wanted one thing for myself. I genuinely enjoyed it, even when I wasn't winning. It was fun, and if she didn't know, I felt it wasn't hurting anything. I know that sounds stupid." I shook my head. "It just got away from me and I couldn't control it anymore." I felt relieved to admit it out loud.

Pastor Conner sat there silently, nodding as I spoke to show he was listening. "Can I ask you something, Rick?" he asked.

"Sure."

"Why the other night? Why were you so harsh? Cut off? Because you were going to gamble?"

I shook my head. "My gambling problem took a turn for the worse a while ago when I played poker with a couple of shady individuals. I was keeping it from her because we were endangered."

"Sin has a way of leading us down paths we never intend on travelling."

"Yeah. You got a good point there, Pastor." My ear itched and I rubbed it between my index finger and thumb as I asked, "What do I do?"

"You have to rebuild."

"That was seventy thousand dollars! I can't rebuild that account! I've been trying, and that's what got me into the shady stuff!"

"I'm not talking about rebuilding your savings account. I'm talking about rebuilding your marriage."

"I'm old. I can't rebuild." I shook my head and looked off toward the wall. "Susan and I are too old for that kind of thing. Maybe we could do that when we were younger , but I don't see that happening at our age."

"You're old, so you must rebuild," he said, correcting me.

"What?"

"Susan is your wife, Rick. She adores you and always has."

"I don't see that right now," I replied.

"I know," he said. "You have to make her see it with your actions, and you have to tell her everything. Let her know your heart as you just did with me."

"I don't think she'll be receptive, and I honestly don't blame her."

"Come on, Rick. We're talking about Susan Alderman. She's been to every woman's conference this church has ever hosted and has counseled several dozen women in the church over the years. If anyone can get through this, it's you two. Susan's good for it."

"You didn't see how much I hurt her."

"I did. I was there when you left her in the dark. At the hospital, and then at the house, I saw it all." He leaned in. "I also saw a woman who loves you despite all of that. She wouldn't be in pain right now if she didn't love you, Rick."

"If you think it's possible, I'm willing to try. What do I have to do?"

Shuffling the papers around on his desk, he pulled his calendar out from the pile and set it on top. Clicking his pen, he said, "What's a good day of the week to start counseling?"

"Changes weekly. I can just text you what day ahead of time for the following few weeks." I paused. "Well, I'm retiring soon, so really any day is fine."

The pastor set his pen down and his eyes widened. "Really? Retiring?"

"Yep. I got early retirement because of budget cuts."

"That's great news! When's your last day?" he asked.

"November 27th."

"Oh wow, so next month. That's great. So we'll stick to text messages until then."

"Okay. For the next few weeks, Thursday will be fine," I replied, smiling as I watched him mark down the next few weeks. "I'll talk to the wife about coming. I'll do it today."

CHAPTER 16

When I arrived home later that morning, Susan's car was gone. I headed to the back of the house to relax on the deck. It was a little nippy outside, but the cool air was refreshing. Taking a deep breath, I kicked my feet up in front of me and relaxed, settling myself in the chair. For the first time in a while I felt lighthearted and hopeful. The pastor thought we had a chance to work things out. I watched two birds sitting up in a tree in the neighboring yard. They were chirping away as they jumped from branch to branch. A smile came onto my face as I recalled bird watching with little Beth when she was younger. We had a robin make a nest in our backyard, and we spent hours watching the mother fly back and forth between the yard and the nest to feed her young. Suddenly, my phone rang, pulling me from my thoughts.

It was Cole. I said, "Hello."

"Hey. You know Fred Foster?" he asked.

"Doesn't ring a bell. Why? What about him? Who is he?" I asked, sitting up to a more alert position.

"He's a cop. Anyway, he found a lead on your guy, Lincoln."

"Oh, yeah? What'd he find out?"

"He's wanted in a few different states along the western coast. He's a high time drug dealer and a wicked bad guy. Fred wanted your number and I said I'd get back to him on it. Wanted to make sure that was okay with you first. I know how you are about your personal information."

"Yeah, that's fine. Give it to him."

We hung up. Fred called me within a few minutes.

"Alderman?" he asked.

"You can call me Rick. This Fred?"

"Yeah. So this Lincoln guy . . . when and where did you play poker with him? It wasn't in your report."

"Ahh. It was in the Valley at a warehouse. I remember he had pallets of diapers."

"Diapers?"

"Yeah. Diapers." I glanced out to the guest house as I thought another moment about Lincoln. "He also had this bouncer guy, his name was Bear. Big, scary looking guy. Bald with a beard that would make a lumberjack jealous."

"Okay." I could hear him write stuff down on a piece of paper. "He had an RV too. He took me inside that at the casino."

"Which casino?"

"North Bend, the one up in Airway Heights."

"Okay. Did you see the plates or know the model of the RV?"

"No. I wasn't thinking about that kind of stuff. I had a gun pressed into my back. I was trying survive and protect my family."

A crashing sound suddenly came from behind me on

the deck. I turned and looked. It was Susan. She had tripped over a clay pot and shattered it. The flowers and dirt were everywhere. It was a mess. It matched the expression on my wife's face quite well. She had tears running down both sides of her face.

"What was that?" Fred asked.

"Don't worry about it."

"Okay. Rick, is there anything else you can tell me about this Lincoln?" Fred asked.

I kept my eyes on Susan. "No. That's all I know."

"Okay. I'll update you directly on anything we figure out."

"Thanks, Fred."

I hung up with him and got up from my seat. Susan shook her head and started to cry more. "Why couldn't you tell me, Rick?"

I grabbed her arms and said, "I was scared. We were all in danger, and I was just trying to get it to go away."

She shook her head and cried again. After a few moments, she was able to speak. "Why were you able to tell whoever that was on the phone with such ease, but not me?"

"That was a cop. They're going to find him and put him away. They have resources and can do something besides worry!" I began to say. "It was to protect you, Susan." I looked her deep in the eyes to help communicate to her my passion as I continued. "They knew about Beth and the grandkids." I shook my head as my eyes welled with tears. "I had to do it the way I did. That's all there is to it, Susan."

She walked past me and sat down in one of the chairs on the deck. She folded over into her palms and cried.

"What can I do to fix this?" I asked, coming over to her and resting a hand on her shoulder. "Just tell me what you need."

She looked up at me with tears in her eyes. "Never have done it to begin with?"

"That's not even possible!" I snapped at her. Guilt immediately crushed me at my harsh tone. I tried to retract my anger, but it was too late.

"You're never going to change," she said with a soft and hopeless tone. It hurt.

I took in a deep breath and focused on my breathing. *Keep breathing. Stay calm to think clearly, like Ron said.* Thinking about my time with the pastor earlier that morning, I looked at her.

"Pastor Conner reminded me that I need to love you like my own body. The passage in Ephesians. Somehow, I had gotten so wrapped up in myself that I had forgotten to show you how much I care for you, and I'm going to work on that." I continued to rub her shoulder as I bent my knees to get at eye level with her. "I love you, Susan."

"You talked to the pastor? When?" she asked, startled.

"This morning, and I went ahead and set up counseling every week with him for the both of us."

"I'm not going," she replied bluntly. "There's no reason."

Someone could have busted my knee caps right then with a baseball bat, and I'd welcome the pain from it compared to the way Susan made me feel in that moment. I was devastated. "Really? No counseling?" I asked.

She shook her head. "We're too old. We're not just a couple of young, dumb kids with years ahead of us."

"Well, I'm going with or without you . . . but I would

love for you to join me." Standing up, I left her on the deck and went inside when she didn't say anything else.

Susan kept herself cooped up in the guest house for the rest of the day. Making use of my free time, I did a few loads of laundry and repaired the leaky faucet in the bathroom. By the time the dinner hour rolled around, I found myself hating the silence in the house. I headed down to Heidi's diner to see if I could catch Ron and have dinner there.

When I got inside the diner, I was surprised by how packed it was. Every seat up at the bar had a butt in it, and there was only one empty table in the whole establishment—and that was only because a man and a woman were getting up to leave.

Still at the door, I watched the couple make their way to the register to pay for their meals. Penny was there, taking their money.

"What's going on?" I shouted toward Lucy over the noise of the restaurant.

She looked up from the register and flashed a smile. Pointing up to the wall behind her, I glanced up at the sign. It was prime rib night. Twelve dollars got you a ten ounce slab of meat and a baked potato. Smiling, I nodded to her. "That explains it."

She pointed over to the empty table and said, "Take a seat, Ricky. I'll be there in a bit. I got two tables with food ready and then I'll be over, so don't get huffy." She handed the gentleman at the register his change and receipt.

"Understood," I replied. Weaving through the restaurant and around the servers, I made it over to my booth. As I took a seat, a small child—maybe two or three—popped his head up from his seat in the booth next to mine. His little eyes stared blankly at me. His mom told him to turn around and I grinned. It made me think of Beth being that age all those years ago.

"Coffee?" Penny asked, coming up to my booth a few minutes later.

"Nope. Going to have dinner." Looking up at her, I saw past her and into the kitchen through the serve window. It was a different cook. "Where's Ron at?"

"He took the night off," she said, seeming to be holding back.

"What's going on with him?" I asked, looking intently into her eyes. "He okay?"

"He's okay," she replied. "Just a cold or something."

"Yeah. Crazy he's missing prime rib night."

"Yeah, he'd be here if he could. So what'll it be?" she asked, pen ready to write on the pad in her other hand.

"I'll take the Chicken Parm. To go."

"Not staying?" she asked as she put the pad away without writing on it.

I smiled. "That's what 'to go' usually means, right?" We both laughed. "No, I'm not staying. I'm going to see Ron."

"He's living with his son, Brackon, F-Y-I."

"When did that happen?" I asked.

"Back a few months ago. He wanted to spend more time with Emmy and Joy and figured that would be the best way to do it."

"Okay." I stood up. "How long on that chicken parm, you think?"

"I'll get it done quick for ya." She left my table and

headed to another table. I watched for a moment as she grabbed their empty soda glasses and headed up to the front to the server's station.

I walked over to the register and leaned against the door frame that led out of the diner as I waited for my meal. Looking across the lively restaurant, I thought about Ron. I sure hoped he was okay. I watched families and other patrons enjoying their meals, and it made me smile knowing that Ron was responsible for building such a wonderful place.

Not long after, probably fifteen minutes or so, my food was ready. Penny brought it out of the kitchen in a white plastic sack. She set it down on the counter and I stepped up to the register to pay. She rang it up and took my money. As she handed me the change, she said, "Take care of yourself, and tell Ron he'd better get to feeling better."

"The other cook not that good?" I asked half-jokingly.

She said, "He's fine. He's just no Ron McCray."

Smiling, I put the change in my pocket and tipped my chin to her as I grabbed the plastic sack off the counter. "Have a good night, Penny."

The drive over to Brackon's house was a bit unnerving. Ron was the closest thing to a father figure I still had in my life. I prayed on the way over that he was really okay like Penny insisted he was. My plate didn't have much room for extra drama. It was already spilling over the edges like an over-stuffed turkey on Thanksgiving.

Pulling up to Brackon's house, I turned off the car and headed up the walkway to the house. The house wasn't in a nice neighborhood, and it fit right in with the other dives on the street. The burned up grass in the front yard was a clear indicator to me that Brackon hadn't changed since I last saw him five years ago at a barbecue that Susan and I were invited to by Ron. Something drove me nuts about the guy, and really any person that lived life aimlessly. People like him always make me think of leeches. They move from host to host and leech off whatever victim they can attach themselves to. Brackon was a special kind of leech. He attached himself to Ron and the government. Ron paid his rent and bills while the government kept him fed. There wasn't any problem with people who need help here and there, but he was one of the people who abused it.

Ringing the doorbell, I could hear the chimes play through the house and the dogs in the backyard started to bark. Footsteps shuffled across the floor and the door opened. Shielding his eyes from the sun, Brackon stood on the other end of the screen door looking like he'd just woken up. No shirt, hair a mess, and what looked to be a fresh scar going across the top part of his left shoulder. And you can't forget the dumb grin on his face. The kind that just makes you want to haul off and punch the guy right in the jaw.

"Brackon," I said.

"Hey, man. You're the firefighter dude. You like save people and stuff, right?" He ran his fingers through his hair, pushing it back.

"Yeah . . ."

His eyebrows furrowed as he must have recalled the barbecue right then. I had wrestled the bottle of vodka from his hands and thrown him on the ground after he backhanded the girlfriend he had at the time. "What you doing here?" His voice was sharp and annoyed.

"Your pops. He here?" I asked, glancing over his shoulder.

"What business do you have with him?" he asked, tipping his chin with an air of arrogance about him.

"It's not business. It's personal."

"Who is it?" Ron asked in a holler from a room down the hall. His voice was faint, but I could tell it was him.

I opened the screen door and pushed through Brackon's arm that he had raised up to block the doorway. "It's me, Rick," I shouted as I walked down the hallway.

Ron said, "I'm down here. Second door on the right." I went to the doorway and glanced in the partially open door. Through the opening, I saw Ron sitting in a rocking chair. He had a checkered black and red wool blanket draped over his lap and he flashed a smile as he saw me.

"Hey, Ron," I said, pushing open the door as I entered the room. I sat down on the edge of the bed nearest to the chair he was in.

"Hey, Rick." He looked me over and said, "What you

doing here?"

"Wanted to check in on you. Penny told me you were here. How are you?" Hearing footsteps outside the doorway to the room, I looked over to see Brackon leaning against the doorframe, looking annoyed that I was there.

"Leave us, Son," Ron said with a narrowed look at Brackon.

"The girls will be home soon from their sleepover. So don't get too comfortable in that chair, old man." He bolted down the hallway.

"I'm sorry, but I don't like that kid," I said, looking back at Ron.

"He's a chump. But I love those kids of his." He rocked a little as he brought his hands to his lap and brought them together. "To answer your question— I'm doing good, Rick. You don't need to worry about me."

"Why'd you come to live here?" I asked.

"The kids. Penny didn't say that?"

"She did, but it's a little suspicious that you'd move in here. You're getting old. I just thought—"

Ron laughed. "If I needed help, I wouldn't have

come to my son's house. He's the furthest thing from helpful."

"That's true."

"How'd the shady people like the car?" Ron asked.

I shook my head as I dipped my chin to my chest. "It was all going to work, and then the cops showed up—"

"What, why?"

"Cole. He followed me and tried to help."

"Oh jeez."

"Yeah. They caught the kid, but Lincoln's on the run. Luckily we have some cop buddies helping out."

"That's good. Where's the car now?" he asked.

"Sitting in my driveway. I can bring it by anytime you want."

"Don't worry about it. I wanted you to have it, Rick."

"You sure? It didn't work out with the deal. You can take it back."

"Keep it and do whatever you want with it." Ron smiled.

"Okay," I replied, knowing that arguing with him would do no good.

"Do you think they'll catch that Lincoln character?"

Ron asked as he began rocking softly.

"I hope."

Ron shook his head. "You better watch out."

Fear rattled me at his words. "Yeah, I know. I'm a little worried. I have police watching my house and Beth's, though."

"How's Beth feel about that?" he asked.

"She doesn't know. She's in the dark. I made sure they would be in an inconspicuous vehicle."

"Good thinking."

I shifted in my seat a little on the bed. "So you're okay?"

"Yep. Just a little tired today. Took the night off. I can do that, you know. I own the place." Ron let out a cough, covering his mouth. Then, he asked, "How's Susan?"

"I don't know. She's still upset."

"It'll take some time."

"Yep, and I'm going to counseling."

"At church, I hope," Ron replied, raising an eyebrow. Nodding, I said, "Yes. My pastor is doing it." Shaking my head, I said, "The wife won't join me. She doesn't even live in the same house. She moved into the guest house."

"At least she's nearby. She'll come around eventually," Ron replied with a smile on the corner of his lip. "She's just got to see if you're being *real* or just putting on a show."

"I hope you're right."

We heard the front door open, and little footsteps pounded against the wood floor down the hallway. Then, Emmy and Joy came into the room.

"Grandpa!" they both shouted as they came across the floor and jumped into his lap.

He pulled them each into an arm and smiled. "You girls have fun at Destiny's house?"

I stood up as they started talking to him about their sleepover. I said, "I'll see you around, Ron."

He nodded up at me and said, "Take care."

Leaving the room, I headed down the hallway to leave. As I passed the living room entryway, I glanced in. Brackon was passed out on the couch with the TV blaring. I went into the room and picked up the remote. Turning it off, I saw a blanket hanging over the recliner near the couch and covered him up with it before heading to my car to leave.

CHAPTER 17

A week came and went, and it was time for another session of counseling. I mentioned the counseling session a few times to Susan with no response from her end, but I still hoped that maybe, just maybe, she'd end up going with me. That morning, I sat in my car for thirty minutes staring at the gate that led out from the backyard.

She never showed.

When I pulled into the church that morning, I

noticed a few extra cars in the parking lot. On my way down the hallway inside, I saw people in the sanctuary setting up decorations. There was an array of different colored cloths being draped all over the front of the sanctuary. Blues, reds, yellows and purples hung from rafters and ran down to the baptismal and piano. It looked similar to a scene you might find at a circus.

Walking into the pastor's office, I glanced over my shoulder as I entered. "What's going on in the sanctuary?"

He motioned for me to sit down, and he came around the desk to close the door. "It's for the teens. This Sunday they'll be doing a few skits." He closed the door and took his seat back behind the desk.

"That's right. I remember something in the announcements on Wednesday night about that."

He nodded. "The kids have a lot of fun doing it." He smiled as he continued, "By the way, I'm glad to be seeing you back in the pews again."

I nodded. "I'm trying."

"Good." His eyes widened as he took a deep breath and said, "How are things going? Susan not joining us?"

"I feel like I'm trying to run in five feet of mud. No, she isn't joining us."

"Why didn't Susan want to join us?"

I shook my head as my chin dipped to my chest. "No interest."

"Susan will come around, Rick. Just keep loving her."

"I do love her. That was never a problem."

"The actions have to align with what comes out of your mouth," he replied.

"I know," I replied, looking out the side window of the office. Spotting a tree outside, I noticed a bird landing on it. "The problem is that I don't know how to get back to where we were."

"Get right with God."

"I'm going to church again," I replied.

"Are you reading your Bible and praying?" he asked.

"Of course."

"What are you reading?"

"The Bible. We just went over this."

"I mean what book?"

"Proverbs."

"I see." The pastor shuffled a few papers around on

his desk like he was looking for something. Then he reached into a drawer and pulled out a piece of paper. He handed it to me. It was blank. He gave me a pen next.

"What do you want me to write?" I asked.

"Write down the most important things to your wife."

"You'd have to ask her that question," I replied, setting the pen down.

"You don't know?" The pastor asked.

"I don't see what the point of this is." I pushed the pen and paper toward him and crossed my arms. "Just tell me what I need to do to fix this."

Shaking his head, he said, "This isn't a matter of *fixing.* You have to give your wife what she needs. Can you list her needs?"

"Well . . ." I said, looking at the piece of paper. "I know she needs love."

"Get more specific."

I sighed heavily. "Why do these women have to be so complicated?"

"Wouldn't it be boring if they weren't complex?" he asked. "Thinking on a deeper level isn't something that comes naturally to many of us men. But we force ourselves to think deeply when we care deeply. Do you remember when you led that Sunday school class years ago?"

"Yeah."

"How much time did you prepare for lessons?"

Thinking back that long ago almost hurt, but I was able to recall the late nights of studying the scripture and cross referencing with different passages. "Lots of time."

"What do you think all that time did for your lessons?"

"Made them better."

"Why?"

"I was prepared and knew the scripture and study inside out."

"Exactly. Your marriage, your wife, needs that same attention to detail."

I laughed. "I've been with the woman for over three decades. I know her inside and out."

"Then why are you here?" he asked in a soft and respectful tone.

"Okay. Gotcha."

Pastor Conner leaned across his desk and said, "View it like a task. Like a lesson you're preparing for. You've got to study her."

"How?"

"Well. She's been out of the house for how long?" he asked.

"Couple of weeks."

"What does she do? Where does she go? What's taking up her time?" he asked.

"I don't know outside of bridge club. I know she goes for walks. I don't think she wants me to stalk her."

"I'm not asking you to stalk her, just pay attention and see what she is spending her time on. It's not stalking. It's studying," Pastor Conner said.

"Okay."

We talked for a little while longer and then our session was done. He'd provided me with some decent advice, which was pretty impressive in my eyes. I thought I knew everything about my wife, but I realized it was only on a certain level. It was a hard pill to swallow to accept that I didn't know everything about her after thirty years. It was required, though, especially if I wanted to make things right between us and become reconciled.

Around lunch time later that day, I was eating a sandwich when I saw Susan walking out of the guest house. She headed toward the side of the house to leave. *Here's my chance*, I thought to myself, setting my sandwich down on the plate. I rose to my feet and went to the living room. Pushing the curtain back slightly with a finger, I watched her pass her car and head down the sidewalk. I waited a moment for her to be out of sight and then slipped out the front door to follow her.

Keeping my distance, I followed as I watched my wife walk. I felt a bit creepy following her, and even a little bad, but I wanted so desperately to know her more. My heart yearned to know her, to see her, to understand her.

I followed her to the park that was up about eight blocks from our house. She cut through the grass to a playground with a bench. She sat down. Coming up to the tree behind her, I noticed the leaves were beginning to turn from greens to yellows and oranges. She turned, and I hid myself behind the tree. I could feel my pulse race. Peeking around the tree, I saw that she was reading a paperback book. I pushed my feet up on my tiptoes from beside the tree to catch a glimpse of the cover. There was no seeing it fully from that far away, so I inched closer. Suddenly, she looked back quickly.

"Rick!" she shouted. "You scared me half to death!"

"Sorry," I said. I walked around the bench; she watched as I sat down beside her.

"What are you doing here?" she asked.

"Just wondering what you do when you go for walks."

She raised an eyebrow. "Why?" she asked in a long, drawn out tone.

Shrugging, I turned my eyes to the playground as I spoke. "I care about you. I wondered what you do when you go for walks."

She closed her book and set it down on the bench. I caught the cover this time. It was Redeeming Love by Francine Rivers. "You need to let me go. You can't follow me like this."

"I'm just trying to get to know you again."

"Rick," she said, setting a hand on top my mine. I looked at her. "We know more about each other than one person ought to know about another human being. We've been together for a long time."

"I thought that, too." My eyes looked down at the book on the bench again. "But I didn't even know you came here to read. Or what you did on walks. You've gone on walks for years." Looking back at the playground, I saw a kid go down the slide. "I want to know you."

"Why?"

"I want to make *us* work." Looking over at her, I said, "I didn't tell you yet, but I'm retiring."

Her eyes widened. "Really? Early retirement?"

"Yeah. They're giving me early retirement because of the budget cuts. That's what we were really doing the petition and rally for. I didn't have the heart to tell you. I thought I was possibly losing my pension. I didn't want to add stress to you. It turns out, though, that if I retire early, I can still get it in full and they won't have to cut more guys at the station."

My eyes turned back to the playground. I didn't look at her as I could feel my eyes well with tears.

"Oh. More lies." She sighed.

"C'mon, Susan!" I replied. "I didn't know what the outcome was going to be. I had to wait until I *knew*. It's not the same."

"Okay." She seemed to accept it. "So all that work canvassing didn't do anything?" she asked.

Shaking my head, I looked down at the cement. "No . . . doesn't appear that it did."

Susan placed a hand on my back and said, "You did a good job trying, though."

"Thanks," I replied, looking over at her with a forced smile. She must have realized she was touching me and regretted it, because she retracted her hand the very next moment.

"I'm going back to reading, Rick, so you can go about whatever it is you do with your free time now." She picked up the book and opened it.

"Okay." I stood up and left the park. As I walked through the grass, I thought about the book she had with her—*Redeeming Love*. What was that about? I hadn't ever heard of the book, but the pages and book cover looked worn. She must have owned it for quite some time. When I got back to the house, I looked the book up online and read the description. My desire to learn more about my wife drove me to purchase a copy to read. With Susan being distant with me, I hoped reading what she was reading would be common ground we could connect on.

I downloaded my copy to my tablet and made myself comfortable on the couch with a cup of coffee. My excitement to read quieted as I dug deeper into the story. It was depressing and disturbed me as I read about the prostitute, Angel. About a quarter of the way into the book, I set my tablet down on the coffee table and went to shower. When I came back out into the living room—at about eight thirty that evening—I was surprised to see Susan on the couch with my tablet.

"What are you doing?" I asked, coming up behind the couch from the kitchen.

She set the tablet down and looked back at me.

"Why are you reading this?"

"I saw you reading it in the park. I was interested. Why are you in here?" I asked.

"My photos from when Beth and the kids were here were on the tablet. I wanted to upload them before I forgot again." She stood up. "If you're trying to impress me by reading a book I like, it won't work." She walked around the couch as I finished toweling off my head. Wearing only my pajama pants, I stood there looking blankly at her.

"I wasn't trying to impress you. I'm just interested. It looked like you have read the book multiple times." I saw her eyes wander away from mine, and I'm pretty sure I saw her catch a glimpse of my shirtless chest. But that could have been my male ego playing tricks on me. I missed her so much—I missed us.

"I'm going to bed," she said, leaving through the doors that led out to the deck. As the doors shut, the silence of the house returned. I watched as she went out to the guest house. Hurrying across the kitchen floor, I opened the door.

"Hey," I called out to her.

"What?" she asked as she turned toward me.

"Does it get better?"

"I don't know," she replied with a sad look on her face.

Confused, I said, "What do you mean? Isn't it your favorite book?"

"Oh." She went flush. "Yes. It gets better," she said with a quick response. Hastily, she went inside and shut the door behind her. I grinned as I closed the doors and returned to the living room to continue reading.

CHAPTER 18

At work the next morning, I sat enjoying the sports section of the local newspaper and a cup of morning coffee in the dining hall when Cole strolled in.

"You hear anything more from Foster?" he asked, pulling up a chair.

I set my paper down and took another drink of my coffee, letting the warmth go down my throat and into my belly before I responded. "Haven't heard anything from the guy since he called me the other day."

He nodded and said, "I suspect you will soon. He has a PI buddy he was going to talk to the last time I spoke with him."

"A private investigator? Why's this Fred guy helping me out like this?" I asked, setting my coffee down on the table. "I don't even know him."

Cole smiled. "He's looking to get promoted over at the station, and cracking a case like this will help him look good."

"What kind of case is *this*?"

"Remember? I told you that Lincoln guy is a wanted fugitive up and down the coast—California, Oregon, and here in Washington. He's a big timer that you got mixed up with."

I adjusted in my seat a little.

"Don't be nervous about it," Cole insisted. "He told me there are cops in unmarked vehicles at your place and your daughter's."

Nodding, I said, "I demanded it before I gave them any information." I took another sip of my coffee. "I didn't know he was a big time criminal. I just fear what means he has to screw with my family more.

He had video footage of my daughter."

"That's insane, man," Cole said, shaking his head.

"No wonder you didn't want to share much with me earlier on. These guys probably rattled you pretty good."

"Yeah. I was terrified."

Megan suddenly came into the dining hall and walked over to Cole. "Hi, Rick," she said to me before directing her attention at Cole.

"Hi," I said politely as I stood up to leave.

"You don't have to leave," Megan said. "I was just going to tell Cole something really quick."

"It's all right," I replied. I went to the kitchen and refilled my coffee. I couldn't help but overhear them talking in the other room.

"I'm going to the school to help out, and my phone died on the way in, so I stopped by."

"Okay, love," Cole said.

It was awkward to hear them talking, so I left the kitchen and went down the hallway. Walking into the multi-purpose room, I spotted Ted and Kane glued to the television set.

"Gents," I said, stepping in to the room.

Kane looked over at me and tipped his chin. "Sup, Alderman."

"Just livin' the dream." Looking at Ted, he looked like he didn't even know I came in the room. "What you doing, Sherman?"

"Shh," he replied.

Kane laughed and got up off the couch to come over to me. Kane lowered his voice and leaned into me a little. "We have a meeting today about those changes coming down. You know anything about it?"

I shrugged. "I don't know a thing."

"Oh, come on! I know you know."

I took a drink of my coffee. It took all I had in me not to frown, knowing full well about Gomer getting the cut. I felt bad. He hadn't been there long, but he was a part of the brotherhood. Sure, he got picked on, but he was one of us. "It's going to be a hard day."

Kane's face looked worried as he frowned. "It's Gomer, isn't it? He's canned."

"Can't say," I said.

"Well, he already got an offer over at a Fire station in

Suncrest. He's going to go work out there if he gets the axe." Kane shook his head as he looked down. "It's not right what they're doing."

"It is what it is."

"Cole said he was helping you the other night and couldn't hang out because of it. What were you two up to?"

"No need to get up in the business, McCormick." I went and sat down with Ted on the couch. Ted was strange, but he didn't need a constant flow of communication like everyone else seemed to need.

The meeting was underway, and Cole looked like he was sweating bullets when he walked to the front of the room. Jensen was up there with him, but he looked more depressed than nervous. Brian sat fidgeting in a seat a few rows up from me.

I leaned up and said into his ear, "Calm down, son."

He looked back at me and said, "No dumb comment about me being a rookie?"

I shook my head.

"Now I *am* scared," he replied, looking forward.

Cole cleared his throat. "Okay, guys. You know we lost the battle with the Mayor and the city. I'm happy to report we were able to keep the pensions safe, and they did lax a smidge. But . . ." His eyes fell on Brain. "Gomer—"

"I know," Brian replied before Cole had to say it. He stood up and turned to all of us in the room. "It's been a pleasure working with all of you, and I already have an offer out in Suncrest."

"Forest fighting?" one of the guys in the back said.

"Yeah, mostly. Houses too, though. Suncrest does have a few thousand people in it."

Cole said, "It's the place we took that retreat last year for the men's conference."

"Beautiful place," Micah added.

"On a lighter note," Cole said as Brian sat back down. "We will be congratulating Mr. Alderman for retirement in the coming month. He's elected to take an early retirement package from the station. So give him a round of applause."

Everyone clapped and a few guys behind me patted my shoulder.

"And Mr. Freeman will be taking his retirement here in two years, which is also an early retirement." Everybody clapped for Micah as he stood up. Just then, the fire alarm went off and we all headed for the exit of the training room. Rushing through the dining hall and down the hallway, we made our way to the fire pole.

Down below in the bay, I saw Brian getting his gear on. I tipped him a nod. "That's mighty good of you to come."

"One last time," he replied, smiling.

Getting into the fire truck, we barreled out of the fire station and down the street with the other engine right behind us. The call that came in was for an apartment building down by the Northtown Mall. There were multiple people trapped inside.

Taking lead on the frontal attack, Ted and I set the hose up right in front of the main apartment building that was engulfed in flames. The heat reaching out from the fire was so intense that I could feel the material inside my jacket begin to stick to my skin. I directed the nozzle toward the flames that were jumping out of the downstairs window.

Ted was leaning against my back as I leaned against his for support. It took a few minutes to get the flames to die down before we began making our way to the door of the structure. Cole came running by and headed to the nearby apartment building, where the fire was beginning to expand over into the structure. The flames danced across the rooftop above Cole as he climbed the metal stairs up to the apartment.

"What are you doing, Taylor?" I shouted.

He didn't hear me. He continued to book it up the stairs and to the apartment door. Seeing the flames grow more in that direction, I got on the radio.

"Taylor! That building isn't safe."

"There's a woman in here, don't question me."

"Gomer," I said. "What's your location?"

"Top side of the structure to your right."

Glancing over, I saw Kent dousing the building so flames weren't able to jump. "Get off that roof and come down here."

"Listen to him," Taylor said over the radio.

I saw Brian come down as I continued hosing the

structure in front of me. Switching the stream of water between the inside of the apartment and the rooftop of the structure Cole was in, I continued fighting the fire as I waited for Brian.

Brian ran over to me and I handed him the nozzle with haste, shoving it into his chest to grab. "Be sure to switch between this structure and that one," I shouted as I pointed to the roof.

"Got it," he replied with a nod.

Running up the same stairs Cole had taken, I got on my radio again. "Taylor—location."

"I'm in the kitchen of apartment 887."

"Copy that." Going into the apartment, I veered right and stayed low out of the smoke. The fire had already made its way partially into the structure, even with the water I had been spraying on the roof. The smoke was thick and impaired my vision.

"Call out," I shouted as I made my way to the first bedroom door.

Suddenly, a beam fell from the ceiling. I jumped out of the way as it dropped right behind me. I kicked the beam out of frustration and then continued forward.

Cole came over the radio. "Got her. Heading out the back window of the structure. Ladder on the north side, please."

"I got you, Taylor," Micah said. "Pulling ladder off truck now."

Turning around, I began making my way back out the way I'd come in. My breath was short as I walked out of the doorway of the apartment and onto the cement slab that sat just outside the apartment. I grabbed onto the metal railing outside the apartment to keep myself from falling. I regained my composure and used the railing for support on my way down the stairs.

Ted must have seen me struggling, because he came rushing over to me as I walked away from the apartment building.

"You okay?" he asked, grabbing my shoulder.

"I'm fine," I replied coldly. Pushing past him, I took off my helmet and mask, letting out a wet cough as I headed over to the truck. Sitting down on the back bumper of the fire truck, I looked up at the apartment building. The flames were mostly out by that point. Cole came over to me.

"What's wrong?" he asked.

I shrugged. "I don't know. Just don't feel right."

He patted my shoulder. "Probably dehydrated. By the way, thanks for coming in there."

"It's what we do. No need to thank me." I got up and walked around to the driver's side of the truck. Cole was right behind me. Reaching into the backseat, I grabbed a bottle of water and twisted the cap off. With one giant gulp, I downed the entire thing. I felt better. Smiling, I said, "Just a little dehydrated."

He nodded and went back toward the apartment as he got on the radio. Watching as Cole walked away from me, my eyes bounced from firefighter to firefighter. Suddenly, it hit me: I was getting too old for this. Everyone looked so young. If I could, I would have been home napping right about that time. And that was the first real time that I felt comfortable with the idea of retirement.

Later that evening, I was reading Redeeming Love on my tablet in the multi-purpose room at the station when my cellphone buzzed in my pocket. It was Fred.

"My PI buddy wants to meet you."

"I'm at work."

"Well, can we come over there?"

"I don't think that's going to work."

He paused. He didn't say anything, but his breathing told it all. They had to have found something.

"What's going on?" I asked. "Did he find Lincoln?"

"Well. We aren't sure. We have a Winnebago heading north, but we want to show you a picture."

"Come on over, I guess," I said. "I'll look at it."

I hung up the phone and headed to go find Cole. He was doing dishes in the kitchen. "Fred and his PI buddy are coming over. They might have found Lincoln. I'm going to see if the RV they have a picture of is the same one."

"Okay," Cole replied.

Not even twenty minutes later, the fire station's doorbell rang. I headed down the stairs and to the door. Opening the door, I saw two men standing out on the sidewalk.

"Hi," one man said, stretching out a hand. "I'm Fred.

This here is Duke Macer. He's a PI."

"Hey," I replied, shaking both of their hands. "Come in." Turning to let them in, they declined.

"It'll only be a moment," Duke said. He pulled out a picture from his inside coat pocket and handed it to me. "Is this the Winnebago you saw?"

Taking the picture, I looked at it. It was the one. The slightly broken door on the entryway was a dead giveaway. That was the only distinguishable thing I could recall from that awful night. "That's it," I said, handing it to him. "Why couldn't you send this to my phone? I could have identified it just as easily."

"It's not always a 'for sure' type thing when it's sent to your phone." Duke remained emotionless as he put the picture back in his coat pocket. He looked at me and said, "Plus I always like to get a feel for a person I'm working for. Anyway, we'll cut him off before he makes it to the Canadian border. We'll keep you updated."

"Thanks. To the both of you," I said.

"Catching bad guys is what we do best," Fred replied, beaming with a smile that stretched across his bony jaw line. I could tell he was proud to be involved in the case.

"Hope it works out. I'll look forward to the call."

They left and I returned upstairs and grabbed my tablet off the couch in the multi-purpose room. I went into the sleeping quarters to my bunk. I said my prayers and read a little bit before drifting off to sleep. Within a few hours of my visit by Fred and Duke, I got the call I had been waiting for.

"We got him," Duke said on the other end of the phone.

I sat up in my bunk and let out a "Really?!"

"Shut up!" Kane said from a few bunks down.

"Thank you, so much," I said in a soft voice into the phone. My fears melted away, and I began to feel a weight lift from my shoulders. He was gone. He was finally gone and I finally felt okay. *Thank you, Lord!* I lay back down and was able to sleep better than I had in a long time.

CHAPTER 19

Meeting with Pastor Conner every week for the next several weeks, I found myself getting closer with the Lord again. Susan continued to keep to herself out in the guest house, but I came to terms with it. I was just happy she didn't end up moving when November rolled around. It worried me at first, her staying out in the guest house, but it became the new normal. Our daughter, Beth, found out about the separation when she tried to surprise us with a spontaneous visit. It was awkward, but she came to an understanding even though she didn't like it.

Taking a seat in the pastor's office the Saturday before Thanksgiving, I said, "Think it'll snow before Thursday? Can't believe we haven't even seen a dusting so far," I said as I took off my gloves and warmed my hands by rubbing them together.

The pastor shrugged. "I don't know. Speaking of . . . any ideas on what you'll be doing for Thanksgiving?" I knew what he meant. Was I having Thanksgiving with Susan and the family? He knew just as much as I did—that she had been cold to any of the attempts at reconciliation between the two of us. There was even a little suspicion in both the pastor and me that she was done with me for good. "Oh . . . I don't know. I was thinking about volunteering down at the shelter on Division."

He raised an eyebrow. "You really have come a distance, Alderman." He smiled warmly at me as he leaned back in his chair and set his hands together on his stomach.

"I want to help." I shrugged. "Without much family

or my wife, it's a good way to spend my time. Plus, I'm sure Susan will be hosting some kind of shindig in her guest house. I'd rather be somewhere else."

"Just give her the house to use that day," he recommended.

"That's a good idea. I didn't think about that." Looking over my shoulder toward the sanctuary, I asked, "Need any more help for the Thanksgiving play?"

He shook his head and raised a hand. "Building those lighting poles was plenty enough, Rick. Thank you. You ready for retirement?"

"Ready as I ever will be."

"How many more days?"

"Seven," I replied, grinning.

"What's next?" the pastor asked.

Shrugging, I said, "I don't know. Haven't figured that out."

"You will," he replied. "What else is going on?"

"Got my will done finally. I sat down and just powered through it."

"Good, good. When did you do that?"

I laughed. "Last night. I remembered last night that

you told me to tackle it before I came here today, so I did."

He smiled. "Good. And your daughter? How's she?"

"Doing well," I said.

"Did she and Jonathan get that house?"

"Yep. Escrow closed last Wednesday."

"That was nice of you to sell that car to help them out like Ron suggested to you. You have some good friends, Rick."

"I do, I've been blessed. I really just want to help whenever I can now. It feels good. It's satisfying." The weekly meetings had turned from counseling into just a friendly get-together and fellowship with a fellow believer. We'd spend a half hour to an hour just catching up and discussing whatever came to us. I treasured my pastor's advice and conversation.

Later that day, back at the house, I was reading Redeeming Love for the umpteenth time when Susan came into the house to fetch something. I let out a laugh as I read the scene that involved

Michael, Sarah and the barn.

She stopped and looked over at me. She was over in the kitchen, and I was in the living room.

"What's so funny?" she asked.

"I'm reading Redeeming Love, and—"

She interrupted before I could continue my sentence. "You're still reading that? And what are you laughing about? If you don't like the book, just don't read it! You don't have to be rude about it."

She continued off toward the hallway that led back to the laundry room. I got up and dropped my tablet on the couch to pursue her. Catching up behind her, I said, "I was reading the barn scene with Micah and Sarah. It's funny. As far as reading it, I've read it several times through since I got it. I want to read more like it, but I don't know where to start in the book world."

She stopped and turned to me. Her anger fell away and was replaced by a surprised look. The corner of her mouth curled up in a smile. "That is a pretty funny part." She thought for a moment. "Miriam . . . " She let out a laugh.

I smiled and nodded. "I truly love the book, Susan. I

can see why yours is so worn out."

She turned and continued onward to the laundry room. I followed her again.

"Hey . . . I was thinking about Thanksgiving and   " I began to say.

"I want you to be there, I just feel it'd be awkward, Rick. Could you find something else to do? I know Ron always has that turkey dinner down at Heidi's every year . . . maybe go to that?"

Her words hurt like a serrated knife jammed into my leg and twisted. Pushing the painful comment aside, I said, "I was just going to offer you the house."

"Oh," she replied softly. She looked remorseful for her comment. "I'm sorry I said that. That'd be amazing if I could use the house." She breathed a relieved sigh. "It'd help a ton, actually. I've been worried about how to fit all my family in the guest house."

I nodded. "It's yours."

"Thanks," she replied. "What were your plans?"

"Going to volunteer at a soup kitchen. Figured I'd make use of my time."

"That's generous of you." She looked me in the eyes.

It was one of the few times she had since the split. I saw a glimmer of hope in them. I saw a sparkle of that admiration she'd once held for me. She said, "You've changed."

"I didn't do anything. God did. But yes, I feel different, in a better way. I'm a different person altogether."

She didn't say anything, just nodded.

We parted ways. Leaving the laundry room, I went back to the living room. I sat on the couch and held the tablet in my hands to give the impression I was reading, but I wasn't. While my eyes fixated on the words that lay before me on the tablet, I got lost in my thoughts. I had been with Susan for longer than I'd lived with my parents when I was a kid, almost twice as long. She was all I ever knew when it came to life, and I missed her. My thoughts skipped over to retirement, and then leaped over to the pastor's question—what's next?

I didn't know.

I closed my eyes and bowed my head. I prayed for God to help me know what to do next. I put all my trust in Him in that very moment.

CHAPTER 20

Thanksgiving Day came too fast. When I woke up that morning in my bed, it reminded me of every Thanksgiving we'd ever had in the Alderman household. I could smell the sausage, onions and celery cooking downstairs in the kitchen. Getting out of bed, I made my way down to the kitchen. Susan was nice enough to even brew me a pot of coffee.

She turned to me as I walked in smiling. She grinned

over at me from the stove. "Good morning."

I went around her to the coffee pot. "Thanks for the coffee. Sure feels like old times," I said, pulling a cup down from the cupboard.

A smile crept from one side of her mouth as she continued pushing the sausage in the skillet around in the pan. Looking over at me as she tilted her head slightly, she said, "Yeah. It really does."

I took a seat at the kitchen table and began thumbing through the black Friday ads. Toys, clothes, waffle makers and more toys flooded the colorful, full-page ads. "Doors open at six pm Thanksgiving day?" I asked with a laugh under my breath.

She looked over at me. "Yeah . . . every year they get more ridiculous. Not sure why it's still considered *Black Friday* when it's on Thanksgiving—a Thursday!"

I continued through the ads. "It truly is ridiculous." We shared light conversation for thirty or so minutes. It was enjoyable. I suspected that she reciprocated the feeling, because even though she was done prepping the stuffing for the turkey, she lingered in the kitchen a bit longer than needed.

A text came through on my phone. It was the contact I had down at the Division's soup kitchen. He needed me to come in right away since one of the volunteers called in sick.

I told Susan about it and then went and put on my favorite sweater. It was a dark gray sweatshirt, rather boring by anyone's standards, but it was special to me. Susan had bought it for me last winter after my last one got left behind when we vacationed to the hot springs in Idaho. I didn't even ask her for a new one. She just bought it and surprised me with it one day when I came home from work. It was these little moments that I missed the most since she had left. She had a way about her that kept everything running smoothly in life. "I'll see you around," I said on my way through the kitchen to leave.

"Okay." She turned back to what she was doing before whipping around again to face me. "I'll put some leftovers for you in the fridge."

"Thanks," I replied with a smile. I left out the front door and headed to the soup kitchen.

Walking into the soup kitchen, I immediately saw the speaker from the men's breakfast that I had spoken harshly with. I felt an overwhelming need to make amends with the man. I strolled across the smooth cement floor and over to him just as he was leaving a table he had been talking with.

"Hi," I said as he turned around and saw me.

He smiled.

"I wanted to apologize to you," I said. Shaking my head as I looked down, I continued. "You were right about blind faith. Man . . ." I let out a laugh. "Our lives are so driven by trusting God fully and being blind to the future. I've learned that so much lately, and I'm sorry for what I said."

He nodded and put his hand on my shoulder. "I'm glad you came around, and thank you for the apology."

"No problem. I'd better get going. I'm helping out here. Gotta find this guy that I'm supposed to meet here."

"Named Jake?" he asked.

"Yeah." I tilted my head slightly. "How'd you know?"

"That's me, Rick!" He laughed.

A smile broke out across my face. "Wow . . . I didn't even remember your name." I went flush.

"Don't be embarrassed, it happens to us all sometimes."

"Okay," I replied. He showed me over to the serving stations and helped me get set up. As I began to serve, my eyes scanned across all the tables and the people that were at them. Some of the people looked normal—I'd never guess they were needy if I saw them on the street. Others looked needy. It broke my heart to see so many people there on Thanksgiving Day getting food, but I also felt extremely blessed to be part of their lives, if only for a meal.

It was tragic, yet at the same time, beautiful. So many people were in need, and a dozen or so people were there to help fill that need.

I met and served a multitude of people for the next few hours until the second shift came to help. After saying my goodbyes, I left to go check on Ron at the diner. On my way over to the diner, I reflected on my time at the soup kitchen. The people I met had real problems. Instead of worrying over a pension, they worried over where their next meal was coming from. Instead of being concerned about how much they had in their savings account, they worried where they were going to pillow their head every night in winter in order to live another day. It helped to shape my perspective and give me a deeper understanding of how really petty and small my problems were in light of others.

When I arrived at the diner, I wasn't surprised to see it busy. Ron's deep fried turkey was one of the best meals I have eaten in my life, second only to my wife's turkey. Everything she did, made, or had a part in was just a little bit better than anything else in life.

Penny wasn't there. It was one of the other ladies that worked there, Ally. She greeted me when I walked in the door. I took a seat up at the bar top and declined the menu she offered me.

"You going to have the Thanksgiving meal?" she asked.

I nodded and looked over her shoulder toward the kitchen's serve window. "Ron back there?" I asked, glancing at her.

"He is. But he's a bit busy. Bet you could slip back there and say 'hi,' since it's Thanksgiving and all."

"I'll do that," I replied, getting up from the barstool I sat on. Coming around the bar, I went through the swinging doors to the kitchen.

There he was. His hands moved like a blur as he ran three different burners and worked on slicing turkey all the same time. He didn't even notice me standing there for a few moments. Looking up at me, he grinned, but the smile fell away. He looked disappointed and asked, "Why aren't you home with Susan?"

I leaned against the pillar that sat in the middle of the kitchen and let out a long sigh. "Things aren't so hot with her. I've been trying."

"Try a little harder." He laughed. "You'll get there."

"I don't know, man. She's pretty cold about the idea. I've been doing counseling with the pastor and she's still not coming around."

"You made her pretty mad with all this, eh?" he asked, looking up for a second as he paused for only a moment from cutting slices of turkey.

"Guess so," I replied, letting out a breath of air from my lips that revealed the defeat I felt inside.

Adjusting my feet, I said, "I gave her the house for Thanksgiving . . . let her host all the family she wanted to have over."

"Isn't it your family too?" he asked, continuing to fill plates of food and toss them up into the serve window.

"Nah. All my family is back in Arkansas. The ones I have left, anyway."

He nodded. "What you been up to?"

"I was at the soup kitchen helping out today."

Ron stopped what he was doing entirely and stared blankly at me. "*You* served at a soup kitchen, Rick?"

"You're making me nervous, Ron. Go about what you were doing, it's not that profound."

He continued his work as he spoke. "No, Rick. That is quite profound for you." He looked at me and shrugged to his side. "No offense."

"None taken." I knew I'd been rather selfish for most of my life, and it wasn't until I really started getting close to God again and relying on Him that I saw that light.

"So what are you going to do? Aren't you retiring soon?"

"Yeah, my last day is here in a couple of days. I don't know my plans yet." Thinking about Jake and the basis of the message on blind faith, I said, "I'm just going to trust God fully and have faith that He will lead me."

"You're sounding like a real Christ-doer, Rick."

"What's that?"

"Doing what Christ would do. Remember when He was sweating blood in that garden? He struggled, but He poured his faith into God and trusted."

I nodded.

Ally popped her head through the double swinging doors and said, "Rick. You got someone here for you."

"Weird. I didn't tell anyone I was coming here," I said.

Going out through the double-swinging doors, I

froze when I saw Susan standing near the door of the diner. She looked like an angel. She had on her black and white pea coat and a pair of red gloves. Her hands were clasped together in front of her, holding her white purse. She was wearing the red Cloche hat that I had bought her a few winters ago for a fireman's ball we had attended. She was absolutely breathtaking.

Slowly, I made my way over to her, coming close so I could hear her over the noise of the diner.

She cleared her throat, looking nervous as she said in a soft and delicate tone, "Rick."

"Susan."

"I've spent quite some time trying to locate you. Is your phone off?"

I reached for my pants pocket and it wasn't there. "Must be in the car."

She looked nervous as her eyes bounced around behind me. She was looking all over the diner. Using the brim of my index finger, I pulled her chin delicately to look at me. "What is it, dear?" I asked. She looked into my eyes so deeply that I could feel our souls touch.

"You don't know this . . . but I've been meeting with the pastor too." She touched my arm. "Don't be mad at him. I told him to keep it from you. I didn't know if this was really what I wanted. I needed to work on me first."

Even the chilliest November on record in forty years outside couldn't keep my heart from melting at my wife's words.

She smiled for a moment and then said, "I want you to come home." The six sweetest words I had heard all day. Heck, in months, even years, maybe.

"Okay," I replied, nodding without hesitation.

"I want to make this work, Rick. Please take a minute and think about it," she insisted. Disbelief at my answer was clear on her face.

Looking into her frightened eyes, I softly grabbed her cheeks, pulled her in close to me, and kissed her. My heart swelled with so much love, emotion and happiness that I could barely stand it. It was ecstasy to taste those lips again.

"I love you," I said, rubbing her shoulders as we released from our kiss. "Of course I want to go home with you."

She smiled, but I could still sense the worry behind those beautiful eyes of hers. But it didn't matter, we were going home together.

CHAPTER 21

Snow began falling as we pulled onto our street.

Leaning up to look out the windshield, I said, "It's the first snowfall." I glanced over at Susan as she held my hand that sat on the console between us. She beamed. She loved the snow. Winter was her favorite season. The quietness that the blankets of white laid across the greater Spokane area was her favorite part of the holiday. It was quiet and beautiful.

"It never gets old, no matter how many times I see it," she said, grinning as she kept her eyes on the flakes coming down in front of our headlights.

"It is beautiful," I replied.

Pulling into the driveway, I saw cars parked all along the side of the curb. I noticed Cole's car was among them. "You invited Cole over for Thanksgiving?" She leaned to see where I was looking and her eyebrows furrowed.

"What's wrong?" I asked.

"He was supposed to park a block down," she replied with a heavy sigh.

"What?" I asked.

Her eyes fixated on the garage door in front of us that the headlights were beaming on. Watching as the snowflakes fell between the headlights and the garage, I waited for her to say something.

She sighed and said, "It's your retirement party-slash-Thanksgiving."

Looking over at Susan, I said, "I'll pretend to be surprised. It'll just be our little secret."

"Okay," she said, smiling. I could tell she was happy. We got out of the car and headed up to the house.

She kept her arm intertwined with mine all the way up to the door. It felt so good to have her back in my arms. Her warmth and her love were coming back to me.

Walking into the dark house, I flipped on a light and everyone jumped out and yelled, "Surprise!"

A few of the kids had streamer poppers and yanked the cord on them, shooting streamers up into the air. I jumped a little from the noise. Cole, Kane, Ted and Micah all had fistfuls of confetti that they tossed up in the air over my head. A rainfall of colors fell across my vision as I looked across at all the people who had come. Even Brian came, though he had finished at the station a while ago. Beth came up to me and hugged me.

"Happy Retirement, Dad," she said, wrapping her arms around my neck. I saw Jonathan standing a few paces back. I smiled at him and motioned him over. He joined the hug.

While the snow might have begun to fall outside for the first time this winter, and the temperature was chilly, my heart was eternally warmed by all the people that had come. Jensen shook my hand after my hug with Beth.

"You've served the city well, and you will forever be known as one of the brotherhood," he said confidently. His eyes glistened for a moment before he patted my shoulder and walked past me.

Laughter, turkey and a heaping serving of good times took us late into the evening as the snow piled outside in the yard and atop the cars. At one point, when everyone went outside to let the kids run around in the snow, Susan pulled me aside into my study upstairs. Sliding the door shut behind her, she looked at me. Those pretty eyes still seemed to be hiding some amount of fear behind them.

"I started that counseling with the pastor once a week last month. I'm trying to trust you. I want to trust you, but you hurt me so badly that it's going to take time. I don't want you to ever hurt me again, Rick. Can you promise me that?" she asked, coming closer to me. "Tell me everything is going to work out."

I put a hand on each side of Susan and looked deeply into her eyes. "I'm never going to hide anything from you again. I promise."

"Why do I still feel like you could be lying?" Her eyes began to water. "I thought you saying something like that would make me feel better, and I don't. I'm scared, Rick." She dipped her eyes into her hands, and I wrapped my arms around her.

Kissing her forehead, I said, "Stop your solo sessions, or keep them, but make a group session with me, too. We'll fix this, dear, and we'll be able to, regardless of our age, because we'll have God's help. It's going to take time. You have to have faith that it'll work out." I wrapped my arms tighter around her and held her a little bit longer. "We'll have our faith in each other and our trust in God, that he'll bring us through this."

She lifted her eyes to meet mine.

I leaned my forehead against hers as I peered into her eyes. "Our wedding day might be just a series of photos in a scrapbook now, but it'll forever be the best decision I've made in my life, Susan. I love you."

BOOK PREVIEW

Preview of "The Perfect Cast"

Prologue

Each of us has moments of impact in life. Sometimes it's in the form of *love*, and sometimes in the form of *sadness*. It is in these times that our world changes forever. They shape us, they define us, and they transform us from the people we once were into the people we now are.

The summer before my senior year of high school is one that will live with me forever. My parents' relationship was on the rocks, my brother was more annoying than ever, and I was forced to leave the world I loved and cared about in Seattle. A summer of change, a summer of growth, and a summer I'll never forget.

Chapter 1 ~ Jess

Jess leaned her head against the passenger side window as she stared out into the endless fields of wheat and corn. She felt like an alien in a foreign land, as it looked nothing like the comfort of her home back in Seattle.

She was convinced her friends were lucky to not have a mother who insisted on whisking them away to spend the *entirety* of their summer out in the middle of nowhere in Eastern Washington. She would have been fine with a weekend visit, but the entire summer at Grandpa's? That was a bit uncalled for, and downright wrong. Her mother said the trip was so Jess and her brother Henry could spend time with her grandpa Roy, but Jess had no interest in doing any such thing.

On the car ride to Grandpa's farm to be dropped off and abandoned, Jess became increasingly annoyed with her mother. Continually, her mother would glance over at Jess, looking for conversation. Ignoring her mom's attempts to make eye contact with her, Jess kept her eyes locked and staring out the window. Every minute, and every second of the car ride, Jess spent wishing the summer away.

After her mother took the exit off the

freeway that led out to the farm, a loud pop came from the driver side tire and brought the car to a grinding halt. Her mom was flustered, and quickly got out of the car to investigate the damage. Henry, Jess's obnoxious and know-it-all ten-year-old brother, leaned between the seats and glanced out the windshield at their mom.

"Stop being so annoying," Jess said, pushing his face back between the seats. He sat back and then began to reach for the door. Jess looked back at him and asked, "What are you doing?"

"I'm going to help Mom."

"Ha. You can't help her; you don't know how to change a tire."

"Well, I am going to *try*." Henry climbed out of the car and shut it forcefully. Jess didn't want this summer to exist and it hadn't even yet begun. If only she could fast forward, and her senior year of high school could start, she'd be happy. But that wasn't the case; there was no remote control for her life. Instead, the next two and half months were going to consist of being stuck out on a smelly farm with Henry and her grandpa. She couldn't stand more than a few minutes with her brother, and being stuck in a house with no cable and *him*? That was a surefire sign that one of them wasn't making it home alive. Watching her mother stare blankly at the car, unsure of what to do, Jess laughed a little to herself. *If you wouldn't have left Dad, you would have avoided this predicament.* Her dad knew how to fix everything. Whether it was a flat tire, a problematic science project or her fishing pole, her dad was always there for her no matter what. That was up until her mother walked out on him, and screwed everybody's life up. He left out of the country on a three month hiatus. Jess figured he had a broken heart and just needed the time away to process her mom leaving him in the dust.

Henry stood outside the car next to his mother, looking intently at the tire. Accidentally catching eye contact with her mother, Jess rolled her eyes. Henry had been trying to take over as the *man of the house* ever since the split. It was cute at first, even to Jess, but his rule of male superiority became rather old quickly when Henry began telling Jess not to speak to her mother harshly and to pick up her dirty laundry. Taking the opportunity to cut into her mom, Jess rolled down her window. "Why don't you call Grandpa? Oh, that's right... he's probably outside and doesn't have a cell phone... but even if he did, he wouldn't have reception."

"Don't start with me, Jess." Her mother scowled at her. Jess watched as her mother turned away from the car and spotted a rickety, broken down general store just up the road.

Her mom began to walk along the side of the road with Henry. Jess didn't care that she wasn't invited on the family trek along the road. It was far too hot to walk anywhere, plus she preferred the coolness of the air conditioning. She wanted to enjoy the small luxury of air conditioning before getting to her grandpa's, where she knew there was sure to be nothing outside of box fans.

Jess pulled her pair of ear buds out from the front pouch of her backpack and plugged them into her phone. Tapping into her music as she put the ear buds in, she set the playlist to shuffle. Staring back out her window, she noticed a cow feeding on a pile of hay through the pine trees, just over the other side of a barbed wire fence. *I really am in the middle of nowhere.*

Chapter 2 ~ Roy

The blistering hot June sun shone brightly through the upper side of the barn and through the loft's open doorway, illuminating the dust and alfalfa particles that were floating around in the air. Sitting on a hay bale in the upper loft of the barn, Roy watched as his nineteen-year-old farmhand Levi retrieved each bale of hay from the conveyor that sat at the loft's doorway. Each bale of alfalfa weighed roughly ninety pounds; it was a bit heavier than the rest of the grass hay bales that were stored in the barn that year. Roy enjoyed watching his farmhand work. He felt that if he watched him enough, he might be able to rekindle some of the strength that he used to have in his youth.

While Roy was merely watching, that didn't protect him from the loft's warmth, and sweat quickly began to bead on his forehead. Reaching for his handkerchief from his back pocket, he brought it to his forehead and dabbed the sweat. Roy appreciated the help of Levi for the past year. Whether it was feeding and watering the cattle, fixing fences out in the fields, or shooting the coyotes that would come down from the hill and attack the cows, Levi was always there and always helping. He was the son of Floyd Nortaggen, the man who ran the dairy farm just a few miles up the road. If it wasn't for Levi, Roy suspected he would have been forced to give up his farm and move into a retirement home. Roy knew retirement homes were places where people went to die, and he just wasn't ready to die. And he didn't want to die in a building full of people that he didn't know; he wanted to die out on his farm, where he always felt he belonged.

"Before too long, I'll need you to get up on the roof and get those shingles replaced. I'm afraid one good storm coming through this summer could ruin the hay."

Levi glanced up at the roof as he sat on the final bale of hay he had stacked. Wiping away the sweat from his brow with his sleeve, he looked over to Roy. "I'm sure I could do that. How old are the shingles?"

A deep smile set into Roy's face as he thought about when he and his father had built the barn back when he was just a boy. "It's been forty years now." His father had always taken a fancy to his older brother, but when his brother had gone away on a mission trip for the summer, his dad had relied on Roy for help with constructing the barn. Delighted, he'd spent the summer toiling in the heat with his dad. He helped lay the foundation, paint the barn and even helped put on the roof. Through sharing the heat of summer and sips of lemonade that his mother would bring out to them, Roy and his father grew close, and remained that way until his father's death later in life.

"Forty years is a while... my dad re-shingled his barn after twenty."

"Shingles usually last between twenty and thirty years." Roy paused to let out a short laugh. "I've been pushing it for ten. Really should have done it last summer when I first started seeing the leaks, but I hadn't the strength and was still too stubborn to accept your help around here."

"I imagine it's quite difficult to admit needing help. I don't envy growing old –no offense."

"None taken," Roy replied, glancing over his shoulder at the sound of a car coming up the driveway over the bridge. "I believe my grandchildren have arrived."

"I'll be on my way then; I don't want to keep you, and it seems to me we are done here."

"Thank you for the help today. I'll write your check, but first get the hay conveyor equipment put away. Just come inside the farmhouse when you're done."

Roy climbed down the ladder and Levi followed behind him. As Roy exited the barn doors, he could see his daughter faintly behind the reflection of the sun off the windshield of her silver Prius. Love overcame him as he made eye contact with her. His daughter was the apple of his eye, and he felt she was the only thing he had done right in all the years of his life on earth. He'd never admit it to anyone out loud, but Tiff was his favorite child. She was the first-born and held a special place in his heart. The other kids gravitated more to their mother anyway; Tiffany and he were always close.

Parking in front of the garage that matched the paint of the barn, red with white trim, His daughter Tiffany stepped out of the driver side door and smiled at him. Hurrying her steps through the gravel, she ran up to her dad and hugged him as she let out what seemed to be a sigh of relief.

Watching over her shoulder as Jess got out of the car, Roy saw her slam the door. He suspected the drive hadn't gone that well for the three of them, but did the courtesy of asking without assuming. "How was the drive?"

"You don't want to ask..." she replied, glancing back at Jess as her daughter lingered near the corner of the garage.

Roy smiled. "I have a fresh batch of lemonade inside," he said, trying to lighten the tension he could sense. Seeing Henry was still in the backseat fiddling with something, Roy went over to one of the back doors and opened the door.

"Hi Grandpa," Henry said, looking up at him.

Leaning his head into the car, Roy smiled. "I'm looking for Henry, have you seen him? Because there's no way you are, Henry! He's just a little guy." Roy used his hand to show how tall Henry *should be* and continued, "About this tall, if my memory serves me correctly."

Henry laughed. "Stop Grandpa! It's me, I'm Henry!"

"I know... I'm just playing with you, kiddo! I haven't seen you in years! You've grown like a weed! Give your ol' Grandpa a hug!" Henry dropped his tablet on the seat and climbed over a suitcase of Jess's to embrace his grandpa in a warm hug.

"Can we go fishing Grandpa? Can we go today?"

Roy laughed as he stood upright. "Maybe tomorrow. The day is going to be over soon and I'd like to visit with your mother some."

Henry dipped his chin to his chest as he sighed. "Okay." Reaching into the back trunk area of the car, Henry grabbed his backpack and then scooted off his seat and out from the car. Just then, Jess let out a screech, which directed everyone's attention over to her at the garage.

"A mouse, are you kidding me?" With a look of disgust, she stomped off around Levi's truck, and down the sidewalk that led up to the farmhouse.

"Aren't you forgetting something?" Tiffany asked, which caused Jess to stop in her tracks. She turned around and put her hand over her brow to shield the sun.

"What, mom?"

"Your suitcases... maybe?" Tiffany replied with a sharp tone.

Roy placed a hand on Tiffany's shoulder. "That's okay. Henry and I can get them."

"No. Jess needs to get them." Roy could tell that his daughter was attempting to draw a line in the sand. A line that Roy and his late wife Lucille had drawn many times with her and the kids.

"Really, Mom?" Jess asked, placing a hand on her hip. "Those suitcases are heavy; the men should carry them. Grandpa is right."

Henry tugged on his mother's shirt corner. "I think you should let this one go, Mother." He smiled and nodded to Roy. "Grandpa and I have it."

Tiffany shook her head and turned away

from Jess as she went to the back of the car. "She's so difficult, Dad. I hate it," Tiffany said, slapping the trunk. "She doesn't understand how life really works."

"Winnie," Roy replied. "Pick your battles." The nickname *Winnie* came from when she was three years old. She would wake up in the middle of the night, push a chair up to the pantry and sneak the honey back into her bedroom. On several occasions, they would awaken the next day to find her snuggling an empty bottle of honey underneath her covers.

"I know. It's just hard sometimes, because everything is a battle with her lately."

"She'll come around. You just have to give her some time to process everything."

Chapter 3 ~ Jess

Kicking her shoes off on the front patio, Jess noticed a hummingbird feeder hanging from the roof's corner. A small bird was zipping around the feeder frantically. She smiled as she thought of her friend Troy, back in Seattle. He was a boxer and often referred to himself as the hummingbird.

Entering into the farmhouse, Jess glanced around and saw that nothing had changed since she had been there five years ago. The same two beige couches with the squiggly designs on the fabric sat in the living room, one couch on each side. The same pictures of all the family hung behind the television. And even the picture of her grandmother, Lucille, which sat on the mantle above the fireplace, right between the wooden praying hands and the shelf clock. Everything was the same.

Walking up to the picture of her grandma, she looked at it longingly. *Why can't mom be like you were, Grandma?*

Hearing Henry and the rest just outside on the patio, Jess quickly made her way across the living room, through the dining room and through the door leading up the stairwell to her room she knew she'd be staying in. The wood paneling on both sides of the hallway leading upstairs made her laugh. *He has the money from Grandma's life insurance, yet he updates nothing.* It was so old and outdated, but then again, everything was in the house.

Lying down on the daybed that was pushed up against the lone window in the room, she turned on her side and peered out the window. Pushing the curtain back, she could see down the hillside and a faint view through the trees of the creek. She couldn't help but recall playing in it with Henry and all her cousins, years ago.

They would sneak pots and pans from the kitchen when grandma wasn't looking and journey down the hillside with them to the creek. They were *farming for gold* as they often referred to it. Looking back over her childhood, she couldn't help but have a longing for the simpler times. Grandma was alive, mom and dad were together and all the cousins lived in the same city. She hated being forced by her mother's hand to be at the farm this summer, but she loved the childhood memories that came with being there.

Hearing the door open at the base of the stairwell, Jess slid off the bed. She suspected her mother was going to be calling for her.

"Come down and visit with your grandpa," her mother hollered up the stairs loudly. Jess came out of the room and looked down the stairs at her mom.

"You don't have to yell..."

"Just come downstairs and visit, please." Her mother left the door open and walked away. *It was hot up here anyway.* Jess missed a step on her way down the stairs and tumbled to the bottom.

"Ooouuuchhh!" Jess said, grabbing onto the arm that she had braced herself with on the fall. Glancing up, she was greeted by laughter from a rude, but very attractive, brown-haired boy with the bluest eyes she'd ever seen.

Extending a hand to help her up, he said, "I'm sorry, but that was just too funny."

Jess pushed his hand out of her way. "I'm glad my pain can be of entertainment to you." Pushing herself up off the steps, she stood up and looked at him. "Who are you?" she asked curiously.

"I'm Levi. I live up the road and help Roy out with the farm. I know you're Roy's granddaughter, but I didn't catch your name...?"

"I'm Jess... I had no idea other people lived out here our age. How do you stand to live without cell phones and cable?"

"What's a cell phone?" Levi laughed. "I'm

only kidding. You just get used to it." Jess nodded as she proceeded past him.

Entering into the kitchen, she grabbed for a clean glass from the dish rack and poured herself a glass of ice water. Taking a drink, she looked over to the table to see Henry, her mother and grandpa all staring at her.

"What?" she asked.

"Don't be *rude* with your tone Missy," her mom said. "But are you okay? We heard you fall down the stairs."

Jess's back and arm were hurting a little from falling, but she didn't want to let her mother get the satisfaction of nurturing her. "I'm fine, Mom."

"Ok. Well, your Grandfather and Henry are going to fish over on Long Lake tomorrow morning; did you want to join them?"

Jess immediately thought of her dad. In fact, every time she heard the word *fish* since the split, she'd think of him. Even the stupid commercials on television that were just ads for fishing supply businesses triggered it. She and her father would go on fishing trips at least twice a month during the summer, and sometimes even more. Last year, they had entered a fishing competition on Lake Roosevelt and had won first place. They got a trophy and a cash prize. It put them that much closer to their dream of getting a *real* fishing boat, instead of the duct-taped-up aluminum canoe they had gotten as a hand-me-down from Roy. It barely floated.

She was already upset that she had to be at the farm all summer; she wasn't going to give her grandpa or mother the satisfaction of her going fishing with him. They knew she enjoyed fishing, and that'd be a win for their column. "No." She turned to her grandpa and narrowed her look at him. "I won't be fishing at all this summer. I'll wait for dad to get back to do my fishing." Taking another drink of her water, she finished it and slammed the cup down in her frustration, and then exited the kitchen, angered she'd been even asked to go fishing.

Jess knew her grandpa most likely had some hand in her mother's decision to walk out on her father, and it infuriated Jess. He always had a dislike for Jess's dad. Jess thought it had to do with the day when the three of them had all gone fishing together and her grandpa never got as much as a bite on his hook. Yet her dad, in all his awesomeness, reeled in three that same day.

On her way back to the stairs, she saw into the living room that her luggage had been brought in. Unfortunately, the rude boy was sitting on a couch near her luggage. *Oh great, another encounter with prince charming.* As she grabbed her bags, he lowered his newspaper and looked at her beaming with a smile.

"Why do you insist on smiling constantly?"

"I'm happy."

"I find that hard to believe. You live in the middle of nowhere and have, like, no life." Levi kept the smile on his face and brought the paper back up to read. Jess felt like she was a bit harsh with him. "I'm sorry. I didn't mean that. I'm just... really upset right now. Sorry."

"You don't even know me or my life. You're just a city brat and I'm just a country hick, so let's just keep our distance from each other."

"You think I'm a brat?"

"No, I don't think you are..."

"Good..."

"No, let me finish. I know you are a brat." He lowered his paper and glanced at her. "The way you carried on in there with your grandpa was horrible. I wouldn't be caught dead talking to anyone that way, let alone my own grandfather."

Jess shook her head with her tongue in cheek. "You know what? You're right. Let's keep our distance from each other."

Levi raised his paper back up to read, and she scowled at him. Her grandpa came into the living room and said, "Levi."

Setting his paper down, he stood up and walked into the kitchen with her grandpa. Her mom noticed the tension between them as she and Henry came in and sat on the opposite couch from Jess.

"What's that all about?"

"Nothing, Mom. Just a country boy living in a bubble."

"What happened?"

"Well... he laughed at me for falling, for starters."

Henry snickered.

"Stop that," her mom said to Henry.

"And then... he called me a brat."

Her mom couldn't help from smiling, but she covered her face in the attempts to hide it. "I'm sorry, dear... You should try to get along with him though; he's been helping your Grandpa a lot out here."

Jess sighed, shaking her head. *I should have*

just taken that offer of Tragan's. That would have made more sense than being here. "Sure, Mom," Jess replied, rolling her eyes. She and Tragan, her friend in Seattle, were going to room together after Jess had learned of the *summer at grandpa's* idea of her mom's. She figured she was eighteen and could do whatever she wanted; her mom couldn't stop her. But after looking into the cost of splitting rent on a two-bedroom apartment in Seattle, she decided against it. There was no way she would be able to finish her senior year, spend time with her friends and work all at the same time, so she elected to obey her mother. Thinking back on it now, she wondered if she had made the right choice.

Chapter 4 ~ Roy

Standing up from the kitchen table, Roy extended his hand and shook Levi's firmly. Every week, after writing him a check, they'd shake on it. There was no need for contracts or other paperwork miscellanies out in the back country. The people out there were trusted and relied on by their word and their handshake.

"Be sure to tell your father hello for me." Roy retrieved a pocket watch from his pants' pocket and placed it in Levi's hands. On the face, it had an etching of a train stopping to let people on, and the exterior was entirely made of gold. "I want you to have this. I picked it up from the flea market the other day, and when I saw it, I thought of you."

"What about it made you think of me?" Levi asked.

"Life is kinda like a train. Sometimes it stops; sometimes it goes, but along the way it's always on track going somewhere. When my train had stopped, you were there to hop on."

"I'm sorry, but that sounds quite ridiculous."

"Ridiculous or not, I want you to have it."

"I can't take this," Levi said, rubbing the

surface before trying to hand it back to Roy.

"Please take it. I'll be offended if you don't. Now, don't forget to tell your father hello for me."

"I will, sir. It's always a pleasure working with you." Heading for the side door that led out of the kitchen and into the porch, Levi turned to Roy. "You have your work cut out this summer with that girl."

Roy smiled. "I know." Patting him on the back, Roy said, "That's why I have God to help me." Levi nodded and proceeded out into the porch, shutting the door behind him.

Walking through the kitchen, Roy could hear his daughter and grandchildren conversing about him in the living room. Stopping, he leaned against the doorway and listened.

Jess laughed. "He belongs in a home. You know it, I know it... we all have known it since Grandma passed. It's just ridiculous that he's draining his retirement paying that stupid boy."

She sure doesn't like him.

"My dad isn't going to give up this farm, Jess, that's just the way it is. This farm is in his blood. Without it, who knows how long he'd hold on. Meadows down the block from our house in Seattle would be perfect for him... but I don't see it ever happening, and I don't know if I want it to, either."

Roy sighed heavily as he leaned against the door frame. *She's already looked into it?* As if the next minute aged him fifty years, Roy found himself exhausted. Going back into the kitchen, he took a seat at the table and glanced out the large kitchen windows that overlooked the front yard. He watched as Levi walked the sidewalk out to his truck.

"Grandpa?" Henry said, walking into the kitchen.

"Yes?"

"Do you miss your dad?" Henry asked, as he climbed up to a seat at the table. Reaching across the table, he snatched an apple from the bowl of fruit.

"Every day," Roy replied. Over the years it had gotten easier for Roy, not because he'd missed his fatherless, but because he'd learned to live with a hole in his life.

"I miss my dad... a lot," Taking a bite of his apple, Henry had a smile crawl on his face. "He should be back in town when we get back to Seattle though, so it's not *too* far from now."

Roy rubbed Henry's head as he ignored the

comment about Brandon entirely. "Are you ready to go fishing tomorrow?" Henry nodded as he took another bite of his apple. "How big of fish are you going to catch?"

Henry leaped up from his chair. Stretching one arm up as high as he could reach, he said, "This big!"

"Ha," Jess said, walking into the kitchen to the fridge. Opening the door to the fridge, she sighed heavily. Roy didn't keep much food that the kids would enjoy around the house; he had forgotten to fetch some for their visit. That was something that Lucille had always taken care of before the grandchildren would arrive.

"There's soda on the porch, I know how you kids don't enjoy lemonade much," Roy smiled, hoping it would be good enough.

Jess shut the fridge and opened the door leading into the porch. Leaning, she looked out and laughed. "Diet caffeine-free..."

Henry cringed as he heard his sister. "Gross, Grandpa."

"I'm sorry about that. We can get some food and stuff tomorrow. Henry and I will be sure to swing by the grocery store on the way back from fishing."

Jess was going to leave the kitchen, but stopped and looked at her grandpa. "There's really nothing to do out here."

"You could go for a walk on the hill, read, paint, and draw... Really, anything is possible out here if you put your mind to it."

"Cell phones and cable aren't possible, no matter how much you put your mind to it."

"That's true, but those things are just distractions. You have to embrace life out here without all that technology."

"Whatever," Jess said, rolling her eyes as she walked out to the porch.

"She stresses mom out," Henry said, looking intently at his grandpa. "We don't know what to do with her."

Laughing, Roy said, "Who's *we*?"

"Mom and I."

Roy furrowed his eyebrows. "You're ten years old. You don't need to worry about Jess. She's not your concern. That's your mom's territory." Henry nodded and got down from the table. Watching as Henry walked out of the kitchen, sadness overtook Roy. Henry was but a child, and he was attempting to fill a void that only a father could. Roy knew he had a long summer ahead of him, but more importantly, he knew God had a plan in the midst of the chaos and turmoil in those two children's lives.

Looking out the window at the chicken coop across the yard, Roy watched as Jess ventured over to it. It reminded him of Tiffany's fascination with the chicken coop when she was but a child. Back years ago when she was six, she'd go out every morning before breakfast and collect all the eggs. While she didn't have a fondness for the smells that resided in the chicken coop, she loved those chickens and hens dearly.

"How many hens do you have now?" Tiffany asked, coming into the kitchen and leaning her head over Roy's shoulder.

"We have twelve," Roy replied with a smile, watching Jess open the door and go in.

Tiffany took a seat at the table and Roy turned to her. "She's not as lost as you think she is, Winnie."

"You don't know how difficult it is..." Tiffany said, putting her hands to her forehead as she rested her elbows on the table. "She doesn't listen to anything I say, Dad, and she hates everyone and everything except her father and her friends."

Roy placed a hand on Tiffany's and brought

it away from her face. "She's just a teenager. You were there once."

"Nothing like this, Dad."

"I'm sure it's different, but it's still the same. Children go through phases in life and she's going through one right now. You add in the fact that--"

"I know," Tiffany interrupted.

Roy stood up from the table and kissed his daughter's forehead. "I love you, Winnie, and your children are going to be *okay*. Just trust that God is doing a work here."

Chapter 5 ~ Jess

Plugging her nose, Jess took one look around the chicken coop and almost vomited. Straw and feces littered the creaky wood-planked floors. Turning, she pushed the chicken coop door open and almost fell out trying to move quickly.

"Disgusting!" she shouted, tiptoeing out of the coop.

Looking across the yard, she could see her grandpa through the farmhouse kitchen windows. He was waving at her with a big silly grin on his face. She turned away and looked across the field just beyond the coop that held the herd of her grandfather's cattle. The field sat at the base of the hill. Glancing up the hill, she saw the big rocks sitting on top.

Jess and her cousin Reese would trek up the hill and sit on a particular rock, and look down across the vast and open valley. Years ago, their grandmother would pack them lunches and juice boxes to take on their journey up there. They never made it beyond the rocks before stopping to eat their lunches, and one of those rocks was where they would sit and eat every time they went. She and Reese stashed a lunch box with a few baseball cards, a couple of colorful rocks and one Pog slammer. Every summer they'd go and find the same rock and the lunch box. It was like finding treasure every time. *I wonder if it's still there.* She thought as she kept her eyes on the rocks.

Walking back over to the farmhouse, she went into the kitchen where her grandfather and mother were sitting.

"Can I borrow the car, Mom?"

Her mom looked at her phone's time and shook her head. "I need to get back on the road shortly. I am stopping in Spokane for a meal with an old friend."

"Cool mom, thanks again for abandoning us just like you did Dad..." and under her breath, she said, "I hate you." Jess began to leave the kitchen.

"Just a minute there, girl! That's not respectful of your mother. If you could be a bit nicer you might be able to take my work truck," Roy said.

Jess stopped, frozen in her tracks. It was a pivotal moment for her. She had to decide whether or not to accept the offer from her grandpa. On one hand, she knew that she *needed* a vehicle if she was going anywhere this summer, and that meant using her grandpa's truck. On the other hand, she didn't want to give him the satisfaction of helping her. She didn't want him thinking that his involvement in her mom and dad's split was okay or justified. She was torn.

"Really?" Jess asked. She couldn't come up with anything else to spit out.

"Yep."

"Ok..." Jess said, walking back into the kitchen. She decided to take the generous offer, but she wasn't going to be happy about it. Her eyes searched the counters for a set of keys. "Where are the keys?"

"How about an apology? To your mother?" Roy asked.

Jess's jaw clenched and she could feel her blood begin to boil as she tried to keep herself from screaming. Turning slowly to her mother, she smiled forcefully. "I'm sorry, Mother."

"And what about *me* being kind enough to use the truck?"

Jess's teeth ground a bit while she tried to keep the smile. Without opening her mouth, and through her teeth, she said, "Thank you... Where are the keys?"

"Right there," Roy said, pointing to the counter. There was a stack of mail, a screw driver and some magazines.

"I'm not seeing them."

"The screwdriver," Roy said with a laugh.

"Ohhh...." Jess forced another smile. "I see."

"You don't have to drive it if you don't want to. I'm just offering it. It ain't a beauty by no means."

"No, I understand... I want to drive it." Jess grabbed the screwdriver and darted out of the kitchen. Leaving the farmhouse, she walked quickly along the path out towards the garage when her grandpa opened the window from the kitchen.

"The truck is along side of the barn," Roy hollered.

"Thanks!" Jess shouted over her shoulder. *Ugh... I didn't have to thank him again.*

Coming to the barn, Jess found that the barn doors were opened and she ventured in for a moment. Looking up at the rafters, she was filled with a familiar feeling that had been lost in her childhood. Back then she had such little care for life and the problems of the real world, like high school. Glancing over to the upper loft of the barn, she saw hay bales and recalled building forts with her cousins. They'd stack bales that reached almost to the ceiling of the barn.

Snapping herself out of the memories, she

turned and left the barn, headed for the truck that was parked along the side. When she got to the truck's door, she couldn't get the door open. Kicking it, she began to scream in her frustration. It was so hot outside she could barely hold onto the handle to open the truck for more than a moment. "Come on!"

"Calm down," Henry said coming around the corner of the barn. "You sound like you are being killed, Jess."

"Shut it, twerp."

"Let me help." Henry came up beside Jess.

"Ha. I'd like to see you try," she replied, stepping out of the way of Henry.

Henry gave each of his hands a spit and rubbed them together. *Gross.* She watched as her brother used all his force in the attempts to dislodge the truck door's handle. It was useless. He stopped and began to look around, spotting a wooden rake stuck in the ground as if it had been there for a very long time.

"You are going to rake the truck?" Jess asked jokingly.

Henry remained silent as he dislodged the rake from the ground. It appeared to have sunk partially into the grass and dirt in the field. Brushing off the dirt, Henry came back to the truck and used the butt of the rake to jam it up into the door handle.

"Good try, but I don't—" Suddenly the door popped open. Henry stood proudly with his chest puffed out. "Thanks," Jess said.

"Pleasure helping you, madam."

"Trying to talk like a cowboy," Jess said with a laugh. "Even Grandpa doesn't talk like that."

Henry beamed. "It's fun to pretend."

"I'm sure it is; I use to do the same thing when I was younger. Thanks bro." Pretending and dolls use to be a huge part of Jess's life. All the way up until she hit ninth grade and Suzie Donaldson came over to visit after school one day. Jess could recall it like it had just happened. When Suzie came over, she had laughed at Jess's doll collection. That marked the turning point for Jess. She wasn't going to be a little kid who played with dolls anymore; she was going to be a *cool kid* like Suzie, and leave the dolls behind.

Jess climbed into the truck and shoved the screwdriver into the ignition. After turning the screwdriver over, the truck fired up loudly and she pumped the gas to get it going. "Yay..." she said sarcastically as she began pulling forward around the front of the barn.

"I wanna go, I wanna go!" Henry shouted as he ran alongside the truck.

"I'd love to let you... but I can't." Jess drove off, leaving Henry in the rearview mirror as she went down the driveway, over the bridge, and out onto Elk Chattaroy Road.

Did you enjoy this preview?
*Pick up a copy of **The Perfect Cast** today!*

OTHER BOOKS

Love's Enduring Promise Series

The Perfect Cast (Book 1)

Finding Love (Book 2)

Claire's Hope (Book 3)

Dylan's Faith (Book 4)

Stand Alones

Love Again

Love Interrupted

Visit www.tkchapin.com for all the latest releases

Subscribe to the Newsletter for special

Prices, free gifts and more!

www.tkchapin.com

AUTHOR'S NOTE

When you leave a review on a book you read, you're helping the author keep the lights on. Our books don't sell themselves, it's word of mouth and comments others have made. Simply visit Amazon and/or Goodreads and let others know how the book was for you. It'd help me greatly. Thank you!

ABOUT THE AUTHOR

T.K. CHAPIN writes Christian Romance books designed to inspire and tug on your heart strings. He believes that telling stories of faith, love and family help build the faith of Christians and help non-believers see how God can work in the life of believers. He gives all credit for his writing and storytelling ability to God. The majority of the novels take place in and around Spokane Washington, his hometown. Chapin makes his home in the Pacific Northwest and has the pleasure of raising his daughter with his beautiful wife Crystal. To find out more about T.K. Chapin or his books, visit his website at www.tkchapin.com.

Made in the
USA
Columbia, SC